The Blurry Years

A NOVEL BY

Eleanor Kriseman

Two Dollar Radio
Books too loud to ignore

Two Dollar Radio
Books too loud to ignore

WHO WE ARE Two Dollar Radio is a family-run outfit dedicated to reaffirming the cultural and artistic spirit of the publishing industry. We aim to do this by presenting bold works of literary merit, each book, individually and collectively, providing a sonic progression that we believe to be too loud to ignore.

TWODOLLARRADIO.com

Proudly based in
Columbus
OHIO

 @TwoDollarRadio

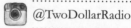 @TwoDollarRadio

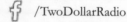 /TwoDollarRadio

Love the
PLANET?
So do we.

Printed on Rolland Enviro, which contains 100% post-consumer fiber, is ECOLOGO, Processed Chlorine Free, Ancient Forest Friendly and FSC® certified and is manufactured using renewable biogas energy.

PERMANENT 100% **BIO GAS®** Ancient Forest Friendly™

Printed in Canada

SOME RECOMMENDED LOCATIONS FOR READING *THE BLURRY YEARS*: Curled up in the window seat of a cross-country flight; at a quiet bar on a weekday afternoon; on the couch in an apartment you're housesitting after you've brought in the mail and watered the plants; in the passenger seat of a sandy car with your feet on the dashboard while someone you love enough to be quiet with is driving you home; pretty much anywhere because books are portable and the perfect technology!

AUTHOR PHOTOGRAPH→ by Jeff Clanet

COVER PHOTOGRAPH→ by Bryan Thomas

The stain of place hangs on not as a birthright
but as a sort of artifice, a bit of cosmetic.

—from *Sleepless Nights* by Elizabeth Hardwick

The Blurry Years

01

We could hear them in the walls before we saw them. My mom said she thought it might be mice. We were eating dinner in bed. We would have eaten dinner in the kitchen but the bedroom was sort of the kitchen too, and anyway we didn't have a dinner table. "Mice," my mom said. "Shit."

I spilled my little cup of spaghetti on the bed. I quickly piled the noodles back into the cup but it was too late. The oil from the margarine left a smear on the sheets. "I just did laundry," my mom said, but she only sounded distracted, not angry.

"What are we gonna do?" I asked her. She shrugged her shoulders. Her mouth was full of pasta. She swallowed. I watched her swallow, watched it go down her throat. I couldn't stop watching her. "I don't know," she said. "Ask 'em to leave?" I didn't want to finish my pasta because it had sheet crumbs and little specks on it from when I spilled. My mom said to finish it or I'd have it for breakfast so I just took it to the sink and rinsed it off instead. It was cold but it wasn't dirty anymore.

The chirping started to keep us up at night. At first I was scared, but then I didn't care because it made me feel cozy. Like we had all the luck, getting to be there together under the blankets, warm and soft while they were stuck scrambling inside the walls. I traced the letters *m i c e* on my mom's back, hoping she'd wake up, but she didn't. So I just listened. "They're in there; we're out here. We are warm and sleepy," I whispered to nobody. I wanted her to wake up but I didn't because I knew she was working the opening shift and she'd be mad.

The noise started to wake both of us up. We stirred when they got real loud, and just as we were drifting back to sleep they'd start dancing and scrabbling in the walls again. "The super won't answer his phone," my mom said to no one. I was doing pigtail braids in the mirror, even though we were already late for school.

My mom was at the counter, making a sandwich for my lunch. "Fuck," she said. "They got into the bread." She held up the bag so I could see from my spot in front of the mirror. There was a big hole in the side, and teeth marks had stretched and spotted the logo. She wrapped turkey slices around cheese slices instead, and poked them with toothpicks to make them stay.

That night we stayed up until dawn, waiting to catch them in the act. "Sit real still," my mom said. "I want to know what we're dealing with." She was pretending like there were maybe just a couple of them, but I was guessing more. We heard them but we still didn't see them and we fell asleep slumped against the wall. In the morning our backs were aching and there was cereal spilling from a hole in the bottom of the box of Fruity O's. I scooped a handful off the top before I threw the rest away. "Keep everything in the fridge from now on," my mom said.

I walked home through the alleys like I did when I wanted to find things. I was good at finding things. My mom called me the treasure queen. Every day on my way home from school I found things. That was how we had the tape deck and the guitar case with the smooth velvet insides that I couldn't help stroking every time I opened it. I found heavier things too but I couldn't take them home by myself.

This time I was looking to build some traps, or maybe some weapons. I pulled at some old pots that were fine except for the enamel was scraped off the insides. I found some rope and a bungee cord that was maybe not garbage, holding two trashcans together, but I thought we probably needed it more. I picked up sticks to test them—good sticks were hard to find, the ones that were straight and thin enough to bend but thick enough not to break, but I found them.

When I got home, my mom's friend Bruce was there. Sometimes he brought me treats, like colored pencils or packs of Juicy Fruit, so I liked him. Bruce was bent over, looking at the place where the walls met the floor. "I think this is where they're coming out," he said. My mom was leaning over too, and she had her hand on his back. I dumped my treasures on the floor, and the pots clanged as they fell. "I'm building traps," I said. "Or maybe weapons. I haven't decided yet."

Bruce smiled. "I think I can take care of this," he said. I sat in the far corner with the knives and the toolkit and some duct tape while Bruce finished plugging up the hole in the wall. "That should do it," he said. "They'll go out the way they came in; they're too smart to die in there." He gave my mom a long kiss on the mouth and told her to call him if she needed to. I could hear him clomping down the stairs in his work boots. I was deciding what to use as bait. I decided on cereal because they'd eaten it before.

My mom didn't say anything when I set up the traps on the kitchen counter that evening, but when she saw what I was taking to bed with us, she said, "No way. You'll kill us all with those—what *are* those things? Were those the kitchen knives?"

I was proud of my weapon. I waved it around like a wand. In the end she said I could keep it as long as I put it on the floor instead of under my pillow. We hadn't washed the sheets yet and my face was resting on the stain from my pasta. It was too dark to see but I could still smell it, salty and oily.

Soon we could hear them, scrabbling and squeaking. We stayed still. We heard tiny scratches coming from inside the oven and the cabinets on the other side of the curtain. Then a pot clattered on the counter and I jumped up, grabbing my weapon from the side of the bed. My mom sat up, half-asleep. "*What* is going on?" she asked. I darted over to the counter and she followed me.

They were shimmering in the colored glow from the traffic lights on the corner, silver and sleek, changing hues as the light switched from yellow to red to green and back again. One was on the counter. Another one peeked out from behind the oven. A little one was catching drips from the faucet in the sink. Their eyes were dots of black paint; their whiskers were fishing line. I wanted to rub their ears but I was frozen, knife raised high in the air. They were shivering. I moved closer, just to look, and they scattered, disappearing into the darkness. My mom put her hands on my shoulders. "I'll call Bruce again in the morning," she said, and led me back to bed.

When I got home from school the next day, the apartment was covered in glue traps. My mom's eyes were bright and darting. Her cheeks were flushed, a perfect pink. She was beautiful. "It's not going to be pretty, these next couple of days," she said. "But we're going to win this battle." I didn't really want to win anymore. I'd untaped my weapon, put the knives back in the kitchen drawer. It was something about how little they were, and how soft their fur had looked. And how they were maybe one big family, lots of little brothers and sisters and one mom who was taking care of them all and when I thought about it that way maybe we could share our cereal with them as long as they were a little bit quieter at night when we were trying to sleep. But I didn't say any of that to my mom because once she had that look in her eyes she was past listening. So we left the glue traps out and ate some pasta and went to sleep.

Little squeals woke us at dawn. A baby mouse had gotten a front paw stuck on a trap, and a bigger one was gnawing on its leg. It was trying to help the baby, trying to make it free, but the baby didn't know that and it must have hurt like crazy, worse than the time my mom got mad and slammed my hand in the door and it swelled up and turned purple. We didn't know what to do so we just watched. My mom had her hand over her mouth. I wanted to cry but I couldn't. The bigger one finally snapped the bone with its teeth and the baby screamed and it sounded more like a tiny human scream than any noise an animal should make. Then the bigger one dragged the baby by the fur on its neck into the hole that Bruce had tried to patch. The chewed-off paw was still stuck to the glue trap. I felt a little sick.

We just lay there in the half-dark for a long time, not talking, listening to each other breathe.

02

We moved in with Bruce a month later. My mom said she loved him. I loved him because he had a dog. Her name was Shadow and she was a shaggy mutt whose fur was the same color as my hair. Bruce lived in a real house with a backyard and everything. He had his own landscaping company, and a big truck with his company logo painted on the side. He didn't cook but he liked to grill and on cool summer nights after my mom got home from work sometimes we would sit outside on the patio while Bruce flipped burgers and flipped the pull-tabs from his beer into the grass. He used to pay me a nickel for each one I could find.

I had my own room at Bruce's. I missed sleeping next to my mom but I liked being able to close my door, to decorate my room with all the drawings I did in art class. I mostly drew pictures of Shadow. Unless my mom was working weekend shifts, no one was there when I got home from school, and I would let Shadow out to pee and give her some water and a treat and pretend she was mine. Bruce used to keep her in the yard at night, but I started sneaking her in before I went to bed, when they were drinking on the couch in the TV room. Shadow was scared to jump up on my bed at first, but I kept patting the mattress and soon she got used to it, started whimpering at the door at night if I didn't let her in. One morning my mom came to wake me up for school and saw Shadow and instead of getting mad she just laughed and then it was okay. I could never tell if she was going to laugh or get angry when I did something and it always made me nervous.

We were out on the patio and my mom was at the table, cutting up iceberg lettuce and tomatoes for a salad while Bruce grilled. I was brushing Shadow's fur. Bruce and my mom were always tired when they got home from work. My mom said she would kill for a job where she didn't have to be on her feet all day, where she didn't feel like all she did her whole life was serve people food. "At least my customers tip," she said, "and I'm not even *making* their food." Bruce said nothing, just added more lighter fluid to the grill. Flames burst up from between the iron bars, and the meat crackled.

"Who's making you dinner right now?" he said. "Who went out and bought your fuckin' ground meat on the way home from my own job, which isn't exactly a picnic for me either. At least you get to be inside all day."

My mom slammed another head of lettuce on the cutting board to get the core out, and the knife slipped off the table and landed on her toe. "Goddamn it!" she shouted, and hopped over to the steps by the back door to look at her foot. "Someone grab me a paper towel, please?"

Bruce kept flipping the burgers.

"Seriously?" She glared at him. "Cal, please? Kitchen?" I dropped Shadow's wire brush and slipped by my mom where she sat on the steps, grabbing a bunch of paper towels and wetting them carelessly in the sink, bringing her a sopping bundle to wipe up the blood.

"Thanks," she said, distracted, then, "Bruce—you gonna

come look? See if I'm dying?" She waved the streaky red paper towels in the air like a flag. "Losing a little bit of blood here."

"Skin's thin on your fingers and toes," he said. "How many times do you think I've sliced my hand open on the job? Surface cut's gonna bleed like crazy even though it's not bad. Go inside and put your foot up. Can't just walk away from the grill here." She didn't respond, but she stood up and made her way inside, unsteadily. I could tell it hurt. I went in after her, feeling like a traitor for not going right away, and Shadow followed.

She was on the couch already, clean paper towels stuffed around her toes, leg up on a pillow. "God, he is such an ass sometimes," she said. I didn't know what to say so I just held the paper towels in place for her. "Grab my drink for me, Cal?" she said. "I left it on the table."

I ran back outside. "How is she?" Bruce asked, then looked at the drink in my hand. "Tell her she shouldn't be drinking if she's bleeding as much as she says she is. I'll bring in the burgers in a minute."

"I don't think she's bleeding that bad," I said, knowing it was the wrong thing to say, not knowing if there was a right thing.

One night when everything was still good, Bruce sat on the edge of my bed before I went to sleep and told me the story of how he'd found Shadow. "And that was it. She sat on my lap on the drive home, whimpering, and I set her up on a towel in the kitchen with a soup bowl for a water dish." Shadow was eight or nine when he told me the story, and I tried really hard to imagine her as a puppy. She was older than me. "C'mere, girl," Bruce said, and patted the side of the bed, and she ambled in, licking his hand. He ruffled the fur on the top of her head. Then my mom came and stood in the doorway, and the light in the hall shadowed one side of her face and made her hair glow. "All my girls in one room," Bruce said. "I'm a lucky guy."

When Bruce left us a few months later, he took Shadow with him. He didn't even say goodbye to me unless you count that phone call he made a week later from his new house. I could hear a football game on the television in the background, and a woman—my mom said her name was JoAnn—saying she was going to the kitchen and did he want another Bud. Shadow barked and my breath caught in my throat and I couldn't talk. I didn't know what his new living room looked like, so I couldn't picture him on the other end of the line. I wondered if the woman's couch was full of crumbs and coins nestled in the cracks like his old one. I wanted him to describe it to me, but all he said was, "I'm sorry, Cal. You know this has nothing to do with you. You're a good kid." I felt like he was looking at the television when he said it.

I missed Bruce a little bit, but I missed Shadow more. Shadow hadn't left my mom and me. My mom hadn't caught Shadow in the kitchen late at night, whispering *I miss you too baby* into the phone. All I wanted to do was call her name and hear the click of her paws on the linoleum, on her way to me. We got to stay in the house until Bruce's lease was up, which wasn't for another couple months. We had the backyard and the real kitchen and I had my own bedroom but now I didn't even feel like sleeping alone. It was hard to sleep without Shadow. At night, I missed the heat from her body. She used to sleep on the inside of the bed, between me and the wall, curled up next to my hip, and I could feel her shift and settle throughout the night, still there when I woke up.

After Bruce left, I heard a lot of things my mom said on the phone when she thought I was asleep. "I don't know, Deb," she whispered, curled up on the couch. "I just don't know what we're going to do when we have to move out." I tiptoed out into the kitchen and she sat up and angled her body in front of the bottle on the side table. "Cal, I didn't know you were still up. Debbie, I'll call you back later." Or the hissing voicemails she left for Bruce. "How's your pretty little JoAnn, you fucking bastard?" Even I knew leaving a message like that wouldn't make me want to come back, if I were Bruce. I wondered if JoAnn drank a lot, if she was nice, if she liked dogs.

I came home from school a couple weeks after Bruce left, expecting an empty house. But my mom was home, drinking a beer in front of the TV. "Bruce is being a shithead," she said. "We're going to get that damn dog back." She looked like she had an idea but not a plan, which made me nervous.

I didn't say anything on the car ride over. I sat in the backseat, chipping glitter polish off my nails. There was an open can of beer in the cup holder and my mom wanted to steal a dog and I was pretty sure both of those things were against the law. It was August and the AC in the car was broken but I was shivering. This wasn't something adults did. Bruce had broken a lot of rules but they were adult ones, ones that got broken all the time, on television and in real life.

My mom drove straight past their house and then circled around again. "Checking for cars," she said. She parked at the end of the block, and we walked down the street like we always did this. Just a mother and daughter walking home from school on a Wednesday afternoon.

My mom knocked on the front door. "They're not home," I said. "Remember, we just checked for cars?"

"I know," she said, in a voice like she thought I was stupid. "I'm just knocking in case the neighbors see." She tried the front door. It was locked, and for a moment I relaxed. But then she walked around the side of the house. There was just a chain link fence, and then there was Shadow, curled up underneath a tree, then running straight toward us. "You're going over first," she said, and held out both of her hands for me to step on. I fell over onto the other side, and Shadow tackled me to the ground, licking my face all over. My mom climbed over next.

"This is disgusting," my mom said, pointing at a pile of dog poop. "Absolutely disgusting. He doesn't deserve this dog if this is how they're going to treat her. Dog shit everywhere." I'd just started using that word, but not out loud, and not to my mom. "Shit," I would whisper to myself when I stubbed my toe, or spilled out the last powdery crumbs of cereal on the kitchen counter. "Shit, shit, shit."

There was a bowl of water by the back door, and another one beside it with a couple crumbs of kibble inside. The grass was nice, like the grass used to be in Bruce's backyard before he left. There were even a couple of trees with patches of shade beneath them. It looked like she was okay. But then I looked down at her pacing back and forth in front of us. It almost looked like she was smiling. "Yeah," I said. "Disgusting." I didn't see any other poop in the yard.

We walked through the back door and right out the front, leaving it unlocked. It was that easy.

Shadow was quiet in the car, and she settled into my lap even though she was too big for it. I moved my fingers through her fur. She seemed fine, but I would still give her a bath when we got back. I couldn't stop smiling, even though I knew we'd done something bad. "Can she sleep in my room again?" I asked.

My mom slowed to a stop at a red light and turned to face me. "Well, that's the problem," she said. "Bruce knows where we live, remember? So she can't actually live with us, not for a little while." I hadn't thought about that, and it made sense, but then I didn't get why we'd taken her in the first place.

"Well, yeah," I said, "but then where is she going to live? And why did we take her?"

"God, Cal, I'm figuring things out, okay! She'll be fine. We took her because that shithead didn't deserve her, that's why. We'll find her somewhere to live. We just have to drive around for a little bit while I think." She shook her head, like I'd said something wrong. Shadow leaned against me, and pressed hard into me every time my mom took a corner too sharply. "Fuck," my mom said softly. "Guess I should have figured that part out beforehand, right?" She laughed.

"Hey! What about Shauna?" she said. "They've already got Tubs. I'm sure Tubs gets lonely during the day, right?" Shauna was my best friend, the only friend I ever really hung out with. Tubs was their black lab. He was old and fat and loved to curl up in the squares of sunlight that came through their living room window. "Let's see what they're up to!" she said, and made a U-turn to head toward Shauna's house.

We walked up to the front door, Shadow close behind us. We hadn't even brought a leash. Shauna's parents weren't home, but Shauna was, and so was her older brother Jack, who answered the door. He was in high school and listened to really loud music and only wore black. "What?" he said, without smiling.

"Hi Jack," my mom said, leaning on the doorframe like she needed it there to hold her up. "Me and Cal were just wondering if you and your family were in the market for a dog."

"What?" he said, and turned away. "Shauna! C'mere! Callie and her mom are here."

"Jack," my mom said, and ran her hand down his arm. "I just thought you and Shauna might want a friend for Tubs." She smiled at him. "Her name is Shadow." *She's not your dog to give away*, I thought angrily. *I want her.*

Jack blushed, turning red like the pimples that dotted his face, and shrugged. "Dunno, I'd probably have to ask my parents."

Shauna ran to the door and hugged me. "Shadow!" she said. "How did you get her back? I thought she wasn't living with you anymore."

"What's going on?" Jack said. We all looked at Shadow and her yellow-toothed grin, wagging her tail furiously.

"Nothing!" my mom said. "We just can't keep her anymore, you know, we'll be moving to an apartment again soon, and it's just not fair to keep her cooped up all day. So we thought you guys might want to take her. Free of charge."

"Uh, I dunno," Jack said. He leaned in so Shauna couldn't hear and said in a low voice, "I think they're kinda waiting for Tubs to kick the bucket." I heard it, but she didn't. He stopped whispering. "I don't think they want another dog. Tubs just shits all over the house and begs under the table."

My mom nodded, and ruffled Shadow's fur. "Uh huh," she said. "Well, just a thought! You sure? She's pretty great." She held Shadow's floppy ears up on either side of her head.

"Yeah... sorry," Jack said. "You should probably go, though. My parents are gonna be home soon." Shauna's parents didn't like my mom that much.

"I get it," my mom said, nodding. "We'll take off. See you soon, Shauna. Good to see you, Jack." Jack closed the door, hard.

We sat in their driveway for a while. "Well, we have a couple choices," my mom said.

"We can bring her back to Bruce, and have her live in that shithole. Or we can give her to a place that will find a really good family for her. What do you think?" I wanted to bring her home with us, more than anything. But Bruce's backyard hadn't seemed that bad. She'd seemed happy there, even before she'd seen us.

"She can't come home with us?" I said, real quiet.

My mom sighed like I was stupid. "Where do you think he's going to look first, Cal?" She turned around to look at me from the front seat. "He doesn't deserve her," she said. "We don't really have a choice."

"Then I guess we give her to someone else," I said quietly. I was getting it now. We hadn't stolen her for me.

"You're damn right," she said. I was trying not to cry. We drove for a little while then pulled into the parking lot of the Humane Society. "Give her a kiss before we go inside!" she said. She unclipped Shadow's collar and shoved it inside the glove compartment. "Remember, we just found her, right? We don't know her." I nodded.

"She's a sweetheart," she said, as we made our way to the door. "Someone'll pick her out right away. Cal, I swear we'd keep her if we could." We walked inside, Shadow trotting along after us. It smelled like pee, and there were whines and howls and barks coming from the back. And my mom just left her there like it was nothing.

Shadow didn't get it. The woman at the counter had to hold her back when we turned to walk away. "It happens sometimes," she said, apologizing to us. "They latch on to whoever's kind enough to bring 'em in."

Bruce came by late that night. He didn't even knock, just barged in. He still had keys. "Where's my fucking dog?" he yelled. My mom was dozing off on the couch. I was in my room. "I let you stay in this house for free and you go and steal my fucking dog. What's *wrong* with you? Where is she?"

"I don't know what you're talking about, Bruce," my mom said, in a sleepy voice. "Did something happen?"

"Yeah, my fucking dog disappeared out of my backyard, that's what!" As Bruce yelled, I heard his footsteps coming closer and closer.

"Don't you dare wake up my child!" my mom screamed, but she didn't follow him. My door swung open, and I blinked as he flipped on the light.

"Damn it!" he said, his anger deflating. I guess he was expecting to see Shadow curled up next to me. "Cal, you haven't seen Shadow, have you?" I was too scared to tell him the truth.

"No," I said, eyes wide, biting my lip.

He sat down on the side of my bed and started to cry. "I'm sorry, Cal," he said. "I'm so sorry." He covered his face in his big hands and wept at the foot of my bed. I didn't know what to do so I just patted his back for a while. "I'm going crazy," he said. "I'm sure she just got out, I just had this..." He shook his head. "I'm so sorry I woke you up. Go back to sleep. I'm gonna go drive around the neighborhood and see if I can find her." I heard him apologize to my mom, and the front door open and close. I closed my eyes but the knot in my stomach was getting bigger and bigger.

My mom tiptoed in and lay down beside me. "We sure got him, didn't we!" she said. "He'll never find her."

"Yeah," I whispered. There was something about my mom that made me always want to be on her side even when it made me feel guilty. "Yeah, we got him good."

She drifted off next to me, on top of the covers, and I pretended the warmth of her body beside me was Shadow until I finally fell asleep.

03

I was halfway to school when I decided I didn't feel like going. I didn't have to, not really. If I wasn't in homeroom, someone from the office would call the apartment and leave a voicemail for my mom, who would already be at work. When I got home, I could erase the message before she had a chance to hear it. She wouldn't care but I didn't tell her. I didn't do it often but I'd done it before.

I liked school. I liked the beginning of the year especially, when everything was new. I liked lining up my pencils on the side of the desk next to my plastic sharpener with the clear catchall for the shavings. Having clean, new erasers to turn over and over in my hand, the cursive Pink Pearl logo rubbing off from the warmth of my palm. It was just the people that sometimes I couldn't be around. The teachers who were nicer to me after the first parent conference. The girls who went to the mall after school. The boys who ran through the halls, slamming shut the open lockers with the palms of their hands. I couldn't figure out if I wanted to be one of them or be friends with them or if I just wished they didn't exist. If I didn't have Shauna to talk to, I didn't think I'd ever feel like going.

I changed directions and started walking away from school on a side road off of Platt. The sun beat down hard on the part of my shoulders my backpack straps didn't cover. I could feel them reddening already. I liked getting tan so I never wore sunscreen, but I hated the clusters of freckles on my shoulders. A truck slowed, then stopped beside me. I kept my eyes to the concrete. The tinted window rolled down slowly, and a man slung a hairy arm out the open window and waved me over. I stayed where I was on the sidewalk. A trickle of sweat slid down the small of my back. I reached beneath my shirt and wiped it away with one finger, keeping my backpack away from the dampness of my back so my tank top wouldn't stick to my skin. I didn't have anything on underneath. I wasn't wearing bras all the time yet. My mom rarely did, except to work, where she said she'd get in trouble if she didn't. I felt as if I were in a movie. The colors of the day were too bright and vivid for real life—the starched white cotton of his sleeve, the searing red of the car door. I felt like I was watching myself on a screen, acting, waiting for my cue.

"Aren't you supposed to be in school?" a girl's voice said. I looked up. Tanya was leaning over the man in the truck, waving at me. Tanya had worked at The Colonnade with my mom until the manager's girlfriend caught him and Tanya messing around in his car in the parking lot after work and made him fire her. That's what Dell, one of the other waitresses, had told my mom. Tanya was trouble, she said. Tanya had long hair that she could put in a bun using only two chopsticks. She was short, but she always wore sandals with huge cork platforms. After she put on lipstick, she would stick her pointer finger in her mouth to make sure none of it got on her teeth.

Dell had told me once that my mom bragged about me, that she said I was "no trouble at all." I didn't say anything when Dell told me, but I had felt a blush rising to the surface of my skin that I couldn't help, like trying to push yourself under the surface of a pool and floating back up to the top despite your churning.

They were waiting for me to say something. "It's a holiday," I said, and immediately regretted it. The man smiled. The sidewalk shimmered in the late-morning heat.

"A holiday, huh?"

"It's not actually a holiday," I said, crossing one leg in front of the other. "I didn't mean to say that. I was going to go." I slung my backpack off one shoulder as proof. "I have all my stuff with me." I looked up at them.

"Get in," Tanya said. "I'll take you back home. It's hot out. Don't worry, I won't tell your mom." I exhaled. Sometimes it felt as if my life was just a series of moments where I hadn't realized I was holding my breath until I let it out. Tanya hopped out and folded the seat back for me to climb behind. "This is Jeremy," she said.

The music was loud and I was working on keeping my face blank like I didn't care about anything and also trying to figure out who was singing until I realized we weren't heading toward my apartment, that Tanya didn't even know where I lived. "Um," I said quietly, but neither of them heard me, so I said it again. "Um, I didn't tell you my address?"

Tanya turned to Jeremy and I saw an expression appear and disappear like a shadow on the side of her face. "Your mom won't be home till later, right?" she said. "If she's still working the mid-shift." She was. I nodded. "What are you gonna do at home all by yourself?" she said. "Come hang out with us! We're going back to our place." I was uneasy. I couldn't figure out what she wanted from me. When you couldn't tell what somebody wanted from you, it was hard to know how to behave. Tanya seemed like she was trying to be my older sister but also kind of like she was making fun of me.

I was in the car. I was way too far from home by now. I didn't have a choice. "Sure," I said. "But I want a burger first." I said it tough, trying to disguise how helpless I felt. She laughed.

"Sure, we'll get you a burger," she said. "There's a Burger King right by Jeremy's. Fries?" I relaxed a little bit. This was fun. She was right. This was better than being home alone. I didn't care why they wanted me around.

I sat with my burger and fries, recovering from the sting of Tanya asking if I wanted a Happy Meal, which they didn't even sell at Burger King. I was too old for Happy Meals and she knew it. I wiped my greasy fingers on the backseat in silent revenge. My cheeks burned. We turned right off Hillsborough onto a small road, and immediately Jeremy swerved right again, into a parking lot. It was one of those apartment complexes so big that the parking lot was like a maze, twisting left and right and opening up to paths that just led to dead ends. He pulled into a spot and stopped when the wheels bounced off the curb. "We're here," Tanya said. I looked at the dashboard before Jeremy turned the car off. My mom would be at work for another six hours. It was fine.

The apartment was heavy with the smell of smoke, a smell I'd recognized but hadn't known what it was until then. I didn't smoke any weed with them because Tanya said my mom would kill her if she ever found out but I was glad, because I was a little scared to try it. I sat sandwiched between the two of them on the couch, our warm thighs touching as they passed the bong back and forth over my lap, bubbling and exhaling and coughing and laughing. The television was on in front of us, but it blended into the background—I couldn't understand any of the words anyone was speaking, and the image kept flickering and changing too quickly for me to keep up with it. It felt safer to stare at the coffee table where my feet were propped up, at my sandals and the dirt underneath my toenails, at the magazines and sketchpads and Ziploc baggies and piles of change and pencils, at the mugs stained from paint and coffee, the crusty plates that a line of black ants was idly crawling over.

"Oh, shit, I think she's getting a contact high," Tanya said, laughing. "We should stop, Jeremy."

"Nah, she's okay," he said. Everything seemed as if it was in motion, and it felt better to stare at something slow, something still. I didn't know how to say that in words, suddenly, but it didn't worry me.

"I'm okay," I whispered, and put my hand on Tanya's thigh to reassure her. It was so smooth. My legs were tan, and covered in blond hair you could barely see. I hadn't ever felt like shaving my legs, though I'd watched my mom do it a million times before going out on a date or to the beach. But I had just been thinking about how they looked. Not about how smooth they felt. I ran my hand all the way down her leg to make sure the whole thing felt that way.

"What are you doing, you freak?" she said, laughing, but not in a mean way. "Jeremy, she's totally high."

"Can I shave my legs?" I asked.

She shrugged. "Sure, I guess."

I sat on the rim of the bathtub with my legs near the faucet as Tanya ran the water. The fluorescent light was bright, and I closed my eyes so I could concentrate on how everything felt instead. The cold smoothness of the porcelain seeping through my shorts, the warm water blasting onto my legs, the lightness of the shaving cream as Tanya sprayed it into my open palm. Tanya nudged me, and I opened my eyes reluctantly. She handed me a disposable razor from a pack underneath the sink. "I'm not gonna do it for you," she said. I gripped the razor and drew the blade slowly up my leg.

When I got home, I erased the message on the answering machine, climbed into bed, and fell asleep. I woke to my mom standing over me. "I'm going to Daryl's for dinner. You comin'?" I slipped into my sandals and followed her out the door and downstairs to the parking lot.

It was hard to remember the times before Daryl had been around, back when my mom was dating Bruce. Now Daryl was over or my mom was at his place or we were all there. Daryl's trailer was much smaller than our apartment, which wasn't big. I didn't know you could fit a life into a place that small. His younger brother Marcus lived with him, but he didn't make much money, my mom said, so he had to sleep on the couch. It was supposed to be temporary but he'd been there ever since my mom started dating Daryl and it didn't seem like that was changing anytime soon.

Daryl played drums in a band, the kind of band that played at weddings. They did other shows where they played their own music, but those were usually free. His arm muscles were huge from lifting his drum kit in and out of the pickup truck. My mom liked to wrap both of her tiny hands around his biceps and say, "Flex." Then she'd smile like she was proud of him, but also like she was proud of herself.

There was a grimy fish tank in the trailer, on the table by the couch where I sat with Marcus while Daryl and my mom fought in the bedroom. *You shouldn't have driven over like that*, he said, and she said, *I just had a beer to relax after work; it's not a big deal.* He said, *But Callie is in that car with you. You just don't think sometimes.*

Instead of listening to them I tuned out and listened to the water trickling into the fish tank. It sounded like trying to pee in the middle of the night, when only a little bit comes out at a time. Marcus's sheets were bunched up in a corner of the couch. My mom and Daryl got louder, and Marcus said, "Let's go outside." I didn't talk to Marcus that much, but he was always nice to me.

My mom's face was stony when they finally emerged. She swung the door hard, but Daryl caught it before it slammed. I was propped on the edge of the truck bed with the back flap folded down, swinging out my newly smooth legs to kick Marcus, because I felt like kicking something, but only softly. I also wanted someone to notice. The mosquitoes were humming around my thighs, whining and buzzing close to my ears.

I sat on my mom's lap in the front of the truck, seatbelt stretched over us both. Marcus didn't come. Sometimes he rode his motorcycle with us and sometimes he stayed home. We were just picking up pizza from Little Caesars, anyway. All four of us ate outside, on the picnic table that swayed whenever anyone stood up.

When my mom and Daryl started arguing again, Marcus got up and motioned for me to come with him. He took me around to the back of the trailer and showed me the ladder that led to the roof. I'd never seen the ladder before. The rubber coating on the roof was smudged and dirty, but Marcus lay down on it, so I did too. "Look up," he said. There were hardly any trees in the park, and no big buildings close by. "The sky is so clear tonight. You can see Venus. There!" he said, and pointed to a brighter dot in the sky, sounding more excited than I'd ever heard him before. I didn't know much about Marcus even though it felt like we'd known him and Daryl forever. He didn't talk much, except for when his girlfriend Kelly was over. But while my mom and Daryl fought, the sound of their voices but not the words themselves carrying up to the roof, Marcus showed me constellations, drew his finger in the air and made imaginary lines so I could understand how every star connected. We stayed up there until we couldn't hear them anymore.

Back at our apartment later that night, I sat on the lid of the toilet and ran a finger lightly from my ankle to my thigh. My mom hadn't asked about school. I climbed onto the lid, high enough to see my legs in the mirror, and executed a shaky twirl, eyes glued to my reflection. Tanya and Jeremy's apartment felt like a dream, or a memory from years ago. In bed, I slid my frictionless legs back and forth, back and forth, under the blankets. I swam between the sheets. I fell asleep on my back, trying to burn the image of the night sky into my head.

04

I couldn't stop thinking about Marcus and Kelly after that night. Kelly was a hostess at the restaurant he managed. She wore her hair in a French braid like it was part of the uniform. The morning after I'd met Kelly for the first time, I'd tried to teach myself how to French braid using a makeup mirror angled to face the bathroom mirror so that I could see my handiwork from the back. I couldn't get all the wisps from the front to stay in the braid, and I took it out before I left for school.

Kelly always looked like she'd come straight from work, and mostly she had, in her black skirt and button-down, and she always smelled faintly of garlic, complaining about it as if it were much worse than it was, laughing about how she'd have to shower before they went out if they decided to go to a bar after dinner. Just like so many of the other women I knew, I wanted to be like her, but Kelly I wanted to be like because I couldn't figure her out.

Maybe it was the way Marcus reacted to her. He didn't talk much in general, but around Kelly he was chatty, he made jokes, he put his hand on her shoulders or knees when they were really into a conversation. But when he did it, it didn't seem like they were about to kiss or anything. It just made me feel like maybe I hadn't understood what they were talking about, after all. Like there was another layer to the conversation I couldn't yet unlock, something that would come—when? When I was a little older? I wanted to know it now. I got straight As in school. I knew what all the words they were using meant, or most of them, anyway. But it was like you got to be a certain age and then you could say something that sounded normal to everyone else in the room and became a secret code to the person you really wanted to be talking to. I sensed it, but I didn't know how it worked.

It was different than the way my mom and Daryl talked. I knew when they were trying to keep something from me—they were sloppy, loopy, laughing hard or, worse, doing that whisper-shout thing that was more frightening than an actual fight. My mom and Daryl always sounded like they had something to prove to each other, like every conversation was something you had to win, points you racked up to use against the other person later on. Listening to Marcus talk was different.

Dinner had been fun until suddenly it wasn't anymore. Marcus had brought aluminum trays of lasagna and spaghetti and Caesar salads from work, soda in Styrofoam cups. Daryl bought beer and we brought rum from home and Kelly was there too, even though she hadn't brought anything. I ate until my stomach hurt. I loved lasagna. The bottle of rum had been half-empty when we brought it over, and both Kelly and my mom had been pouring it into their Styrofoam cups all through dinner. So I wasn't surprised when my mom tipped the bottle over her cup again and poured out the last of it. She raised her eyebrows. "Well, we sure made quick work of that," she said.

"Probably a good time to switch to beer, anyway," Daryl said, beginning to stand up. "Here, I'll get you one." I could see what he was trying to do but I knew it wouldn't work. I knew better than he did just how stubborn she could be.

"The liquor store's just a couple minutes away," she said, trying to make her voice calmer than she felt, her clenched jaw giving her away. "I'll be right back."

"Really, Jeanne, we're good for tonight," Daryl said.

"It's my fucking weekend tomorrow and I'm going to enjoy it," she said back to him, as if they were the only two people at the table. "Anyone need anything while I'm out?" She got up and started walking fast to the car. Daryl followed right behind her.

A couple minutes later, she peeled out of the parking lot, Daryl in the passenger seat. She'd won this time.

Marcus stood up, putting the tops back on the half-eaten trays of food, gathering our plates and napkins into an uneven stack. "Be right back," he said, and walked inside. Kelly followed after him.

I sat alone at the table for a minute, then decided to bring in the rest of the trash from the table. Kelly had left the door ajar, which I noted with a little satisfaction. Mosquitoes got in when you left the door open. I always closed the door. Before I could push it open further to go inside, I heard Kelly's voice, whiny and insistent, and I froze right where I was. "Come *on*," she said. "Your brother's gone. We have time."

Marcus sighed. "I was just bringing in the dishes," he said. "Let's go back outside."

"You sure?" Kelly asked, dragging out that last word in a way that made me uncomfortable. She giggled.

"Kelly, you know I want to," he said. "Not now. We can't just leave Cal out there alone."

"You shouldn't have to be responsible for her," Kelly said.

"Yeah, well," Marcus said. "Someone should be. And it's not her mom, that's for sure." I blushed, stinging with embarrassment, but a small thrill ran through me at the thought of Marcus taking care of me.

I kept listening, but neither of them spoke for a minute. Then, before I could move, Kelly pulled open the door and almost walked straight into me. "I was just bringing these in," I said quickly, but she didn't look at me like I'd been eavesdropping. It was as if I couldn't have even understood their conversation, as if I were just a child, too young and dumb to even worry about revealing anything in front of.

05

The gas station bathrooms were always open, but if it wasn't the middle of the night and we had a choice, I liked Dunkin' Donuts better. The bathrooms there were cleaner and, if I crossed my legs and sort of hopped around, the people behind the counter would usually let me use it even if we didn't buy anything. If we stopped for the night, we looked for a 7-Eleven, or someplace else that was always open, because it was safer to park there. My mom would only sleep at night if she thought it was safe. Sometimes we drove all night and parked during the day. She'd sleep then, but I never could, even with a blanket over my face to block out the light.

If my mom was in a good mood when we passed a *Welcome* sign, she'd pull over so I could stand beneath it. The signs were always much bigger than I expected them to be when I got up close. *Welcome to Ocala. Welcome to Gainesville. Welcome—We're Glad Georgia's On Your Mind*, with a giant peach in the corner. That was the first state line. Back in Florida, she pulled over at the sign for the Suwannee River so I could look over the railing at the water. It made me dizzy; the river was a long way down.

We were headed to Oregon to stay with my grandma June for a little while. That was all I knew.

I kept asking questions at first. "Why do we have to pack so quickly?" "Why aren't we saying goodbye to anyone?" "What about school?" I stopped asking when she wouldn't answer. We were both quiet for a long time.

The only time I complained was on that stretch of highway after Nashville when we'd just passed the rest stop and the AC had switched off again and wouldn't turn back on even when I hit the dashboard and I kept asking her to turn around so I could use the bathroom but she wouldn't turn around and instead she pulled over and made me pee in the sawgrass on the side of I-24. When I got back in the car, still damp between my legs because we didn't have any toilet paper, I said, "I wish we'd never left home."

"Me too," she said, and turned up the radio.

It was weird how looking out the window of a moving car made me forget about a lot of things. I barely thought about my friends. I'd had plans to walk to Falk's with Shauna later that week to buy a new pair of sandals. I barely thought about starting seventh grade, even though that was all that me and Shauna could talk about before we left. Every time something like that popped into my head all I had to do was stare out the window for a little bit and it would just float out again. The only thoughts that stuck were the ones of home. My mom and Daryl at the kitchen counter, a bottle of anything between them, hysterical with laughter over something I pretended to understand. The frayed, pilling fabric of the couch that I picked at absentmindedly while watching television. The ceilings that looked like popcorn somebody had painted over. No matter how fast everything was going by outside the window, those thoughts didn't go away.

She'd switched on my light, grabbed my suitcase from under the bed, and started pulling clothes from my dresser before I'd even sat up. "What's going on?" I asked, narrowing my eyes against the sudden brightness. She was drunk. Ever since the Fourth of July when she'd drifted off at the wheel, she hadn't been drinking, at least not around me. But that night she was drunk.

"Take your favorite things," she said, tugging hard on the bottom drawer of the dresser, the one that always stuck. "We'll come back for the rest later. Just take what you want. Quick." The drawer came unstuck, sending her stumbling backward. I was half-asleep and obedient, and filled the suitcase easily. Tank tops. My white denim shorts. A soft, old shirt of Daryl's that my mom used to sleep in. Underwear. Flip-flops. My copy of *Bridge to Terabithia*, page folded down to mark my place, which was chapters ahead of where I was supposed to be for summer reading. It was funny, the things I chose to bring, the things I forgot. I brought my toothbrush, as if that were something expensive and irreplaceable. I forgot my friendship necklace—the golden 'BEST' to Shauna's 'FRIENDS,' with the chain that turned my neck green if I wore it for too long.

My mom stabbed at the ignition with the key until she finally managed to get it in. I almost asked her if she needed help but she drove carefully and we didn't go far, just to the IHOP near the interstate. I ate French toast like a robot while she drank a whole pot of coffee and ordered a refill. We stayed until the waitress started wiping the table to move us along, and by then my mom had pretty much sobered up because she didn't ask me to do the tip.

When we walked back out to the car, I noticed the bumper was slightly askew. The glass casing around the right headlight had been shattered.

"What happened?" I asked, pointing.

"Nothing," she said, staring at the car, tilting her head the same way as the bumper. "Nothing happened. Try to sleep in the car. It's late."

Daryl wasn't with us, which was weird. My mom was always with him. But she always spent the night at home, even if she got back really late. We had barbecues a lot at Daryl's place. I would sit on Daryl's bench press machine, part of the outdoor gym he'd put together by scouting out the alleys of the rich neighborhoods on trash nights. He told that story a lot. I'd lean against the metal bar that rose from the bench and fiddle with the screws that held it together while I watched the men light the grill and the women unfold card tables on the patchy grass, setting out sliced watermelon and pasta salad and pitchers of sweet tea.

Memorial Day had been the best. I'd seen my mom walk up behind Daryl while he was turning the hotdogs and put her arms around his waist and settle into his body; and instead of getting mad at her for surprising him, Daryl leaned into her and smiled. In the flickering light from the grill, they'd looked like something I wanted to take a picture of.

Fourth of July had been the worst. I'd been excited to wear my new shorts—red and white stripes on one side, blue with white stars on the other—but they were made of that spandex denim that stretched out so much I had to keep hiking up the waistband to keep them in place. Mom had on a black halter top and lipstick the exact color of pink in the Baskin-Robbins logo. I thought she looked good. So did Daryl. When we got there, he looped an arm around her waist and told her so. But Daryl must have thought Charlene, who was a hostess at the Italian place Marcus managed, looked good too, because I saw him walk up next to her, telling her how much he loved her Coca-Cola cake, his flimsy paper plate buckling under the weight of the food he'd piled on, baked beans slipping off the side and onto the dirt. I walked over to Daryl and Charlene and swiveled my foot back and forth in front of them, making an indentation in the ground. Daryl didn't even notice as I kicked the spilled beans into the hole and covered them with the dirt.

When my mom came back outside with a new coat of lipstick and another red plastic cup full of punch, she saw Daryl leaning into Charlene's story and she grabbed his arm and dragged him behind the neighbor's place. Charlene shrugged her shoulders at Desiree, who was unwrapping packets of sparklers for the little kids. "I'm not gettin' messed up in all that," she said, hands to her chest, palms facing out.

From next door, my mom's voice grew louder and louder until I heard the crack of an open palm on skin, then she came running for me. I'd been excited about climbing up to the roof of the trailer to watch the fireworks, but she grabbed my arm just like she'd grabbed his and speed-walked me to the car. It wasn't even all the way dark yet. On the drive home, I flicked the lock on the passenger-side door up and down until I noticed we were drifting across the centerline.

I grabbed the wheel and jerked the car back into the lane, steering the rest of the way home while my mom worked the gas and brakes. I pinched her arm every once in a while to make sure she didn't close her eyes again. In bed later, I realized there had been no red mark on my mom's face, no handprint. She had slapped Daryl.

The next morning, she came into my room and crawled into bed with me just as the sky was getting light. "Do you think I'm a bad mom?" she asked. I was facing the wall; she was spooning me, still wearing last night's outfit. Her breath was hot on my neck, and I could smell vomit under the minty scent of her mouthwash.

"No," I said after a minute and I meant it, but I knew I should have said it quicker.

In Missouri, my mom decided we had enough money to spend the night at a motel. Just one night. I was so happy to sleep in a real bed. As soon as we got to the room I flopped onto it, the bedspread rough against my bare legs, and turned on the television. I was desperate for something familiar. My mom switched it off.

"Let's go swimming," she said. She tossed a pillow at my face. She got like that sometimes. "We've been cooped up in the car all day." Neither of us had packed a swimsuit. Underwear showed the same amount of body, but it felt different to be in my underwear where anybody could see me. My mom was in her underwear too, but her bra was black and shiny so you couldn't really tell.

Some nights after my mom came home from Daryl's, she would bang into the furniture on purpose or clang the pots together in the kitchen until the noise woke me. She'd pretend it had been an accident. "Now that you're awake, want to walk down to the pool with me?" she'd say. The pool was shaped like a giant kidney bean and sheltered by the different buildings of the apartment complex. It was crowded in the evenings, but when it was really late it would be just the two of us. I would perch on the ladder at the deep end of the bean while my mom swam in restless, sloppy circles in front of me, telling me about Daryl and Marcus and everything I'd missed out on that night.

But at the motel pool in Missouri she was sober and quiet. We were floating in the middle of the pool with our stomachs to the sky, our limbs slowly sinking into the water. "I think you'll like Oregon," she said, and backstroked until her head was floating next to mine, our bodies facing in opposite directions. "It's a good place to grow up. You'll need a real jacket. We'll get you one. Grandma June might have some old ones of mine too." My legs started getting heavy, I kicked a couple times to keep them on the surface of the water. "Does it snow there?" If she answered yes, I would ask more questions.

"Not in Eugene," she said. "Maybe once or twice when I was growing up." I closed my eyes and tried to make myself believe that I was back in the kidney bean. The pool water lapped against the filter, flapping it open, then shut, then open again.

In the room, I showered under such hot water that it left me flushed for hours. My skin was wrinkled and puckered from the pool. My mom washed our clothes in the bathtub and dried them with the hair dryer and in the morning when I put them on they were stiff and smelled of shampoo, but they were clean. At the free breakfast I had bacon and pancakes and used as much syrup as I wanted, and she didn't say anything. Before leaving the dining room, she tossed my backpack under the booth and filled it with whatever would fit. Anything that might stay good for a couple days. Croissants, muffins, packets of jelly, tiny boxes of cereal, waxy green apples and bananas. We didn't go hungry, but I missed certain things. I missed standing next to my mom at the stove, listening to the sizzle of the ground beef hitting the pan, sneaking a lick of the seasoning before she poured out the rest of the packet. I missed the heavy plates with the painted flowers on the rim that I used to trace with my fork between bites. I missed drinking milk in the mornings. But I didn't tell her any of that.

Both of us were in good moods. We'd had dinner at a Dairy Queen in a little town in Nebraska called Grand Island, and that name was still cracking us up because it was the most hick town we'd ever seen and there was no body of water for miles. Grand Island. It was the first time I'd seen her laugh in a while and I was trying to think of more jokes, to keep her laughing. We were going fast on a back road that the man at Dairy Queen had told us would lead to the interstate, belting out our favorite Carly

Simon song. *Jesse, I'll always cut fresh flowers for you.* She was almost screaming it. *Jesse, I will make the wine cold for you.* I was tapping out the beat with my feet on the dashboard. *I will put on cologne, I will wait by the phone for you.* Something about that song made me feel so hopeful, even though it was about Carly Simon going back to someone who didn't treat her like he should. But she sounded triumphant, and I could sense it: Everything was going to work out. Jesse was going to be a better boyfriend this time around. We would make it to Oregon. Happiness fizzed and bubbled up inside me.

We didn't even see anything; just felt a *thump* under the wheels that made us bounce against the seatbelts. Carly Simon kept singing. We hadn't passed another car in miles, but my mom still looked in the rearview mirror before pulling over. She got out of the car, telling me to stay put, but after a minute I went to find her. She was standing over the body of a small animal, staring down, her arms crossed over her body like she was cold. She didn't notice me until I was standing next to her. "Just a rabbit," she said. "Nothing to worry about."

I squatted down. Its body was splayed open, fur wet with blood and its insides were leaking out onto the pavement. Its face was untouched though, and its mouth hung open slightly. Its ears looked soft. I bit my lip. "Can we bury it?"

Mom shrugged. "Sure, I guess. I should get it off the road, anyway."

She dragged it by the ears over to the shoulder so no other car would hit it, and we kneeled next to each other in the dirt beside the tar and started digging. It was so quiet I could hear the scraping of our fingertips breaking the earth.

"I screwed up," she said.

I looked back at the rabbit. The trail of blood from where she'd dragged it gleamed, dark on the asphalt. "It wasn't your fault," I said. "It just ran out in front of the car."

"Not that," she said, digging harder. "I mean, shit, I screwed that up too, but I meant with everything else." The hole was already plenty big enough.

"Like what?" I said. She never talked like this. She unearthed a small stone and turned it over and over in her hand.

"With Daryl," she said. "I messed up pretty bad with Daryl." I wondered what she meant, but I didn't want to interrupt. "With you. I think you're the best thing I ever did and I fucked things up for you—" She laughed and wiped her nose with the back of her arm, and I saw she'd started to cry. "And now we're digging a grave together," she said, laughing harder.

I didn't know why it was funny but I wanted her to think I understood so I started laughing too, and she kept laughing and pulled me close and soon I really was laughing just because it felt good. We sat there a long time, in the dark, just laughing.

06

"God, Callie, it feels like I never left," my mom said, gliding through an empty intersection on a street called Royal Avenue. We had never been to Oregon together, and Grandma June had never come to Florida. Back when she knew our address, she used to send me books at Christmas. She used to call every month. She told me she had my picture on her bedside table. But then my mom started asking her for money every time and she stopped calling.

She called one more time after that; I think when she figured my mom wouldn't be home. "You ever need anything, Callie, you call me, okay?" she said. I nodded, but realized she couldn't see me. "Write this number down, baby," she said. I scribbled it on the cardboard from a six-pack with a marker from my pencil case.

I wanted to call her a few times after that but I forgot to take the piece of cardboard into my room and it got thrown out. I remembered the phone number written on the cardboard just before dawn and ran downstairs in my pajamas, tripping down the stairs in my flip-flops. I would have dug through the dumpster for it but the garbage truck was already on its way out of the parking lot. I walked up to the top floor and watched the sun rise between the buildings, and then I went downstairs in case my mom wandered into the living room and saw the empty pull-out couch.

Grandma June wasn't someone I thought I'd ever talk to again, much less meet. I definitely didn't think she'd want us staying with her. But I hoped that even if she didn't want to see my mom, she'd change her mind if I were there. I wanted to stop driving, even if where we stopped wasn't home. I wanted my world to narrow to one point again, to stay the same in front of my eyes, wanted the landscape to stop blurring as we sped by life instead of living it. We were in limbo. Anywhere with even one familiar thing, one room with a solid floor under my feet, would have felt—if not like home—like someplace I could get used to.

My mom slowed, and made a right down a street that looked nothing like any street in Florida that I'd ever seen. Most of the houses here had small white picket fences around the front yards, and the trees were wide and leafy, no tall palms in sight. "This is it, baby girl," she said, and turned the radio down. She pulled into the driveway of a house the color of a sunburn and parked. "Huh. Her car's not here," she said. She paused. "She's probably at Albertsons. We'll just wait on the porch. Oh, she's going to be so happy to see you, Callie," she said again, but she didn't look like she believed herself.

There was a swing on the front porch, and we swung lazily back and forth while we waited, taking turns propelling ourselves backward with our feet. A silver car pulled into the driveway, and my mom stood up, leaving my side of the swing rocking back and forth. "You stay here," she said. She walked down the front steps, slowly, like she didn't want to make any trouble. A man got out of the driver's seat.

"Excuse me, ma'am," he said, "can I help you?"

She nodded. "Sorry," she said. "I used to live here. Is this still June Willard's place?"

She was trying to act casual but I saw her hands shaking. The man saw me, and his face softened a bit. "You her daughter?" he said. "Sure, I could see the resemblance."

"You got it," she said, laughing like this was her plan all along, like she knew what we were doing. "Can I ask you—do you know where she is now?"

The man's eyes widened, like he understood something he hadn't before. "I thought you were here to see the house, what we've done with it," he said. "I didn't realize—" he stopped. "You don't know," he said, then again, almost to himself. "You don't know."

I ran my hand up and down the iron banister, swiveling one foot on the staircase, looking down at my feet. "I don't know what?" my mom said.

"Shit," he said. "I can't believe I'm the one telling you this. Your mother passed away shortly after we bought the house."

I stopped swiveling. My mom sat down on the steps just underneath me, didn't say a word.

The man ran inside and came back with a cold glass of water. He sat down next to her. "Drink this," he said. "I'm so sorry." She nodded.

I wondered if she was thinking about the motel room we'd stayed in last night, how we'd eaten gas station croissants for all three meals yesterday because they were selling twenty-five-cent two-packs when we'd stopped to fill up the tank with another five dollars, how we'd had to convince the man at the checkout counter that the AC in our room was broken so we'd get a discount. I was wondering where we'd sleep tonight. I didn't want to sleep in the car anymore. I was tired of driving, tired of leaning back the seats and turning off the ignition to say goodnight. I was angry with my mom for driving us all the way here because she'd had a fight with Daryl and she thought her mom could make it all better. I was angry that Grandma June was gone, even angrier than sad. It was harder to feel sad about someone you'd never met than it was to be angrier at someone who was the reason you'd never met in the first place.

My mom started to cry, sitting there on the porch, and I felt guilty. "Would you mind if I used your telephone?" she asked.

"Of course not," he said. "Come on in."

The houses got smaller and closer together and the yards got browner and the sidewalks got bumpier until we pulled up outside of a white brick bungalow that my mom almost drove right by. "Two thirty... three?" she said. "That's it! All right. Just for a couple of days, or a week. I'll find a job. We'll go somewhere else." She knocked on the door.

A woman in a pink silk robe and slippers opened the door. "Jeanie!" she cried. "It's been ages... goodness, look at us! Look at her." She pointed to me. "My god, she's going to be a beauty," she said. "Give her a year or two, you'll be fighting those boys back."

My mom shook her head, but she was smiling. "Starr, you're just the same."

"Well, come on in!" Starr said. "I've got some lemonade, and something to put in the lemonade for the grown-ups, and I've just made a loaf of banana bread. You caught me on one of my days off—I'm not always wearing my pajamas at two in the afternoon. Let's catch up, Jeanie," she said, and hugged my mom again. "Oh, and Russ'll be home later tonight. That's my boyfriend. He's a cop. So don't you worry, you'll be safe with us."

They sat at the kitchen table. My mom asked me to pour lemonade for everyone, and Starr handed me a bottle of vodka for their glasses—"Just a touch more, honey," she said to me, without even looking at how much I'd poured already. I studied their faces.

My mom looked tired, and her hair was greasy from the

halfhearted rinses we'd done in gas station bathrooms. She wasn't wearing makeup, and the circles under her eyes were so deep and purple they looked like someone had drawn them on in crayon. But she was still beautiful, even without trying. Starr was someone who tried. At first it worked, but when she was sitting next to someone like my mom, I could see straight through it. Starr's hair was silvery blond and carefully teased, but the dark roots were just beginning to show. Her cheeks glowed with bronzer, and her eyelids were a shimmery brown. Up close, her mascara was clumped, and her eyelashes were stuck together. Her lips were a pale pink, but they were chapped and slightly smaller than her lip liner made them out to be. Starr was the kind of woman who was truly beautiful when you were squinting, when you let your eyes blur a bit, when you were far away. My mom was the kind of woman who was truly beautiful when you got up close, when you studied her carefully. She held up under my gaze; Starr dissolved.

My mom drank half her glass of lemonade in one long swallow. Neither of them said anything, but I felt like I should let them be alone. I didn't know what to say about Grandma June and I didn't want to listen to my mom talk anymore. I left the kitchen and wandered the dim, carpeted hallways of Starr's house. The car keys were on the front table, and I went out to the car and grabbed both of our suitcases, carrying them in one at a time. *You're welcome*, I thought, and then felt guilty. My grandma was dead. It was okay if my mom sat in the kitchen, drinking with Starr while the day faded.

I curled up on the couch with *Bridge to Terabithia*. It was obvious that something awful was going to happen, but I couldn't stop reading. And I was right. The rope snapped, Leslie drowned; their world shattered just like that. I didn't want to read about death, not while my mom was talking about it in the kitchen. It wasn't supposed to happen to kids, and you weren't supposed to find out about it from strangers. You weren't supposed to swing across a river on a rope you'd used a hundred times before and have it snap off in your hands, mid-swing. You weren't supposed to drive across the country and find out your grandmother was dead and somebody else was living in her house. You couldn't count on anything. Not even in books. I was exhausted. I covered my face with the book, open to the middle, and fell asleep.

I woke to someone shaking me on my shoulder. I opened my eyes and there was a cop standing in front of me. Half-asleep still, I thought I was in trouble until he smiled and I realized it must be Russ, Starr's boyfriend. "You're Callie, I'm guessing," he said. "Starr told me you and your mom were stopping by for a little while." I sat up, dry-mouthed and bleary-eyed. It was black outside.

Starr and my mom were still sitting where they'd been hours before and laughing loudly at things I couldn't overhear. Russ went in to say hello, and motioned for me to follow him when he came back out. He grabbed both suitcases, one in each hand, and walked me to the first door on the left. "Bed's made, bathroom's just down the hall," he said. "Towels are in the hall closet. Starr acts like she's got this place under control but now you know who's really running the show." He winked at me, as if we were in on a joke together.

Too tired to shower, I just changed into fresh underwear and Daryl's old shirt and climbed underneath the heavy pink duvet. From the hallway, I heard Starr slur a *goodnight*. She padded off to the master bedroom at the end of the hallway, and my mom came in. "God, it's good to see her," she said, sitting on the bed and kicking off her strappy sandals. She climbed underneath the covers with me and hugged me close. "We've got each other, Cal," she said. She traced my hairline with her finger. "I'll never disappear like your grandma. No matter how old I am, you'll always know where I am. I'll always help you out whenever you need it." I nodded. She squeezed me extra hard, and then got out of bed again.

I thought she was just going to the bathroom, because she left the door ajar. But she didn't come back in; instead, she joined Russ in the living room, just outside our door.

The television was on, soft enough that I couldn't tell what show it was. "Sorry to bother you," she said. "Can't sleep. Not sure why. I'm dead broke, I've been driving for days, I just found out my mother's dead—I should be sleeping like a baby." She let out a harsh laugh. I sat up, scooted to the edge of the bed.

Russ mumbled something that I couldn't hear. "I'm no good at stuff like this," he said, more clearly, after a minute. "Starr tells me I always say the wrong thing."

"You don't need to say anything at all," my mom said. I wondered how close they were sitting.

I slept half into the next day. I didn't realize how tired I'd been. Starr's house was boring, but it was better than being in the car all day. My mom left early in the morning to buy a newspaper to look for jobs in the classifieds. She was gone when I woke up. I don't know what she did all day, but she didn't get home until after dark. She didn't look happy.

I had this awful feeling one night after the first few days that maybe she wasn't even looking for a job so I looked through her purse while she was in the shower. I don't know what I was expecting to find but all I saw were the classifieds, folded up, with circles around job postings, mostly waitress positions, some secretaries wanted—some were crossed out, some with "call back next week" scrawled on the side. I felt better knowing she wasn't lying, but I was worried. How long were we going to stay here if she couldn't find a job? Did this mean we were going to just live in Eugene now? I wanted plans, promises, something concrete. But those were just a few things on the long list of things she couldn't give me.

I liked watching Starr work. She was a hairdresser, but she worked from home. In the living room, there were two sinks and two professional dryers, and all of her supplies were set up on the bookcase. There were two chairs, with foot pedals to make them go up and down, and a floor-to-ceiling mirror in front of them. The rest of the living room was normal—a couch and a TV and a coffee table.

The loud whir of the dryers was comforting, and I liked listening to the conversations Starr had with her clients. All of the women who came to get their hair done ended up looking vaguely the same—frosty blond, if they weren't already. Farrah Fawcett feathering, which I was learning looked good on some people and not really on others. Starr said she just gave people what they wanted. "I know what's best for them," she told me, after a woman who'd beamed at her reflection one last time in the mirror had left, "but they're happier when they get what they want." She smiled absently, and recounted the money the woman had handed her.

Starr even did my hair once, though my mom wouldn't let her dye it. I'd never had my hair cut at a real professional place. I couldn't believe people paid other people to wash their hair, but after Starr ran the water until it was just hot enough, and massaged my head with creamy coconut-smelling shampoo, I understood why. Her hands worked through the knots in my hair like they were nothing. "You can keep your eyes closed, honey," she said. "I'll tell you when to open." She wrapped my wet hair in a towel and wiped off my face. While she was sweeping up the clippings around my feet, I stared at the girl in the mirror. Me, but sharper.

Starr went to bed before I did almost every night we were there, most of the time before Russ even got home. She always said she was tired. When she wasn't working, she was ambling around the house in her slippers and silk robe, drinking white wine and Sprite—she told me those were called spritzers. She made me one once, and it was mostly Sprite but I could taste the sour fruitiness of the wine underneath when I swallowed. Normally I didn't like the taste of alcohol, because I only tasted it when my mom was so drunk she tried to give it to me, and it was too scary to see her like that, something I didn't want to turn into. But Starr's drinks felt safe. It was daytime; nobody was out of control.

I pretended not to like it as much as I did. People wanted to give you something when you weren't excited about it. Sometimes you had to pretend you didn't want something to get it. So I drank the first one slowly, said it was just okay, acted like I didn't want another. After that, she made me one almost every afternoon with hers. Drinking with Starr made her house less boring. Everything was funny. I felt sleepy, but in a good way. I talked more. And it was like a game whenever my mom came home, to brush my teeth quickly, act normal. I had a secret with someone now.

Starr was like Bambi, sort of unsteady on her feet, trying to make eye contact when you talked to her but looking some-where slightly above your eyes, or off to the side. But she was nice, and she liked having me there. Maybe it was just that she liked having someone there, and it didn't matter who it was. But in the mornings, she'd sit at the kitchen table with me, tracing the silvers and greys on the mottled Formica with her index finger, and ask me about my friends, and my old school, and how I was feeling. None of these were questions it made sense to answer anymore—it didn't feel like we were ever going back. But it felt good that somebody cared enough to ask them.

07

We weren't supposed to stay long. Just a couple of days there. But days turned into a week, and we were still there. Once my mom woke up late, Russ made bacon, Starr made pancakes, we all crowded around the breakfast table. It felt like a family, almost like we were back with Daryl and Marcus again. But most days she left early, came back late.

I woke up whenever I wanted to. I stopped wearing most of the clothes I'd brought with me—if I didn't leave the house there didn't seem to be a point in wearing outside clothes. I said that to Starr one morning and she knew exactly what I meant. "Why do you think I have so many of these?" she said, tugging on her silk robe. "I like to feel dressed up even if I'm not going anywhere. When you work from home, you know..." She padded off to her room and came back with a navy silk robe covered in a pale floral pattern. On her, it was knee-length, but on me it hung lower. "Take off your pajamas," she said. "You'll feel much better in this."

I hesitated for a second, then pulled Daryl's old shirt over my head, standing in the kitchen in just my underwear. Starr held the robe out and I slipped my arms into the sleeves. She tied the strap into a tight bow, then pulled me into the living room to look in the mirror. "Doesn't that feel nicer?" she said. It dipped low, showing my greying white training bra, and it was cold and slippery against my skin, a different kind of comfortable than the frayed softness of my t-shirt. "It does," I said, not knowing whether or not I meant it yet.

When Starr was working, I usually stayed in the living room to watch. Sometimes I'd sweep up the clippings after a client left. I liked to be helpful. When I got bored, I flipped through her books. She didn't have many, just a couple shelves of romance novels with a man and a woman on the cover. They were all the same story over and over, just in a different time or place. There was always one reason they couldn't be together, but they had sex with each other anyway and said they were in love. They acted like they would die if they couldn't be together. I'd never been in love so I didn't know if that was true but I doubted it. Love wasn't like that in real life. But still they made me feel a longing for something I didn't even know I wanted, something I couldn't even name.

Since my mom and Russ both came home late most nights, sometimes Starr would microwave something for dinner, or cook for the two of us. If she was going to bed early she'd hand me a twenty. "Get whatever you want," she'd say.

Sometimes my mom and Russ were so late that I'd gone to bed too, bored by everything on television and sick of flipping through the old magazines Starr kept for her customers. I'd lie in the dark on my back and wonder what we were going to do next. Wasn't Starr going to get tired of us being there? Where would we go?

My mom had said we weren't living in the car, but when we'd slept in there for a week straight, bathed in gas station bathrooms with scratchy paper towels and foamy soap, ate our meals sitting in the backseat, parked in the fast-food restaurant lot, it sure felt a lot like living in the car. It felt like not having a plan. It felt like not knowing.

Those nights at Starr's I stayed up late, and pretended I was asleep when my mom came home and checked on me. I didn't want to talk to her. I didn't think she'd tell me anything I wanted to hear. I let her fuss with the duvet cover and kept my eyes shut and my breathing as slow as I could until she'd walked out of the bedroom again. As soon as I heard her voice in the living room, I climbed out of bed carefully and scooted close to the door, flattening my body against the wall.

"She's out cold," my mom said to Russ. "Poor thing. I know she must be going crazy here. I just don't know where to go next."

"Well, you know you're welcome here," Russ said. "We've got room. We're happy to put you up for a while. I know she likes seeing you. It's good to catch up with old friends."

"I don't know," my mom said. "I know it doesn't feel like a burden now, but it's going to, soon. I don't know what I was thinking. I left all our stuff in the apartment. All we have is what's in your spare room. Shit, the rent's due in a week and I'm all the way across the country with about nothing in my bank account."

"You haven't been back to Eugene in a hell of a long time, according to Starr," Russ said. "How'd you end up all the way down in Florida, anyway?" I couldn't tell if he was trying to change the subject to something a little less uncomfortable or if he was flirting with her. I slid closer to the doorframe, but I was too chicken to peek.

"You really wanna know?" she said. "It ain't pretty."

"Lay it on me," Russ said.

"Modeling." I held my breath. "My mom and I were at the Valley River Center and some man, dressed real nice, suit and everything, came up to us. Said he owned a modeling agency based out of Miami, wanted me to move down there and become a swimsuit model. I was sixteen. He had business cards, classy-looking headshots of other girls my age. Shit, what sixteen-year-old girl in Eugene wouldn't have wanted to live in Miami and be a model? I just left," she said. I didn't know this story. "Wasn't anything else for me here." I thought about Starr. Starr had been here.

"Not what I was expecting," he said. "So you just took off, like that?"

"He paid for the plane ticket—business class to Miami—and I guess that was all it took for me to believe him," she said. "Promised he'd set me up in a luxury apartment on South Beach with other girls my age, that I'd be making so much money I wouldn't know what to do with it. 'Trust me, I know when someone's got it.' I still remember the way he said it."

"So it didn't work out quite the way you thought it would, I'm guessing," Russ said. "Goddamn it. Taking advantage of sixteen-year-olds. What a shithead."

"I was just so fucking bored here—no offense," she said quickly. "I'd never even flown on a plane before. I got in a cab, figuring I could afford it now, told the driver the address. 'You sure that's right?' he said. 'Not the nicest part of town.'"

She fell silent for a minute. I was jealous of Russ, of the way he made her feel like she could tell him anything. She'd known him for a week and already she was telling him something I'd never known.

"God, that house was filthy. Ten girls, four bedrooms, two couches. The roaches. You know in Florida they have these roaches called palmetto bugs? They're fucking huge, first of all, but they can fly too. They were all over that house. We'd smack them out of the air with flip-flops. But we were too high to care that much—we partied—" she stopped here. "I'm drunk, I shouldn't be telling you this. You must think I'm awful."

"No, not at all," Russ said. Then softer, again, "Not at all."

She laughed. "In that case, I won't spare you. My god, we wore the trashiest lingerie for those photo shoots. Garter belts, see-through shit, mesh, fishnets. We just did whatever they told us to. Bent over the white leather sofa, ass to the camera. Crawled on top of the bedsheets, twirling our hair. We spent all our money on coke. Some pure shit down in Miami back then. We were barely breaking even."

"Goddamn," Russ said. I wondered if he was raising his eyebrows, shaking his head.

She kept talking. "I ignored my mom's calls—never answered the phone, always got one of the girls to tell her I was out. When I left, I had enough money for a Greyhound ticket and a couple nights in a cheap motel. I called my mom from a payphone outside the bus station, crying like a fucking baby. My nose was bleeding so hard it was dripping onto my dress, this old denim one, the only one I had that didn't make me look like a stripper. I wanted to come back, start over. But she didn't want me back by then. I don't blame her. I was a fool. So I figured things out for myself. Never left. Until now." She laughed again, the kind of laugh where nothing is funny but silence is worse.

"I think you're being a little hard on yourself," Russ said. "That man was a criminal. Ever think maybe instead of feeling like a fool, you must have been real smart, to have gotten yourself out?"

"That's sweet of you," she said, "but I don't deserve it. I was a fool. Still am, always have been. I never get myself out in time."

They were silent for a minute. I just sat there absorbing everything, my back against the wall, then panicked, thinking maybe she was getting up to come back to bed. I jumped up, dove back under the comforter, waiting for her. But they kept talking, only I couldn't make out their words anymore.

One day I held Starr's kitchen phone in my hand, willing myself to remember Shauna's number, frightened that I could forget something that used to be so vital. I didn't even know what time it was in Florida. Our old apartment, my old school, my friends, everything—it all seemed less and less real, as if when my mom had shaken me awake I'd been in the middle of a dream, and I would never be able to close my eyes and go back to it again.

Another night, another late-night conversation. She hadn't even come in to check on me when she'd come back. I climbed out of bed soundlessly, thankful for the thick carpet, cracked the door, and slid down the wall until I was slumped by the door.

"If you don't mind me asking," Russ said, "why'd you end up coming here?"

She sighed.

"It's okay," he said. "You don't have to."

"No, that's not it," she said. "I'll tell you. I just—god, I feel so fucking stupid. I had a boyfriend in Tampa. Daryl. We were off and on, always breaking up and getting back together. We just couldn't stay away from each other, but the fights got worse. I tried to keep Callie away from it, but I know there were times she noticed something. But I never thought he'd get violent."

I knew they fought. There was that night we left Daryl's Fourth of July party early, when I'd had to steer the car all the way home. But she'd slapped *him* that night. Daryl was never violent. I didn't think. The scratchy carpeting began to tickle my thighs.

"The first black eye wasn't that bad. I covered it with makeup for work, told Cal I'd walked into the doorframe, coming home late. Can you believe that? I would have rather told my daughter

I was blind drunk than admit I'd let Daryl hit me. I thought it'd be the last time. You always think it's going to be the last time."

She'd never told me that. That was because she'd never come home with a black eye. She was lying to Russ. A big lie. I wondered what else she'd told me that wasn't true. What else she hadn't told me. I wanted to see her face so badly right then.

"I see this kind of shit all the time," said Russ. "It's not your fault. It's never the woman's fault. Makes me sick." She didn't respond. "Mind if I smoke?" he said. "You're welcome to have one."

"I don't mind at all," she said. "And I'd love one." My mom never smoked inside. But I was learning how quickly she could shift, how many masks she had. "Anyway, to make a long story short, we had a big fight the night we left. The worst one we've ever had. And I did something really fucking stupid. That's why—" she stopped. "I'm just—I'm afraid to go back."

I held my breath. I still wasn't exactly sure why we'd left. I knew we'd been running from something but I wasn't sure what. I moved closer to the living room doorway, as quietly as possible. I could see them now, my mom's knees drawn to her chest, Russ slouched low, legs stretched out in front of the couch.

"What did you do?" Russ said. "I'm sure he deserved it."

"It's against the law," she said, and laughed, flicking his badge. He was still in uniform.

"I'm not going to turn you in, don't worry," he said, laughing too.

"I rammed his car," she said, sounding almost proud. "I rammed the shit out of his fucking car. I slammed into the back of it with mine before I left. That's why my headlight's fucked. And that's why I'm afraid to go back. I'm afraid he went to the cops."

Pulling my drawers open, lights on in the middle of the night. Pot of coffee at IHOP. The broken headlight, the crooked bumper. It's nothing. Try to sleep in the car. Waking to the sun rising over the interstate. Neck sore, cheek pressed against the window. Closing my eyes, opening them. Not a dream. Pretending not to hear my questions, gripping the steering wheel like she'd fall into a million pieces if she let go.

I was so angry, in a way that scared me. I had the answers to my questions and I was furious.

Sometimes, in the old apartment, I'd get up when I heard the key in the lock, no matter what time it was, and head to the kitchen in my pajamas. I'd have two slices of bread in the toaster before she came in the door. She'd collapse on the couch, with her hand over her forehead. "You're an angel," she'd say. We'd sit together and eat toast with lots of butter, and I'd bring her a cup of water and watch her drink it before we went to bed. One time she'd started crying. "I don't deserve you," she'd said. "What do you mean?" I'd asked. She hadn't answered, just repeated herself, "I don't deserve you." Over and over.

I wanted to take it all back, sleep through every late night, let her be alone with herself. I'd tried to take care of her. But she'd gone and done something stupid again and it was so big that I couldn't fix it. I hadn't even known about it. It wasn't supposed to work that way.

"I doubt he said anything," Russ said. "Sounds like he'd have a lot to answer for as well. You know I can check that, though. See if you've got a warrant out."

"Will you get in trouble?" she asked.

"Nah," he said. "Don't worry about it. I got you."

"You're a good guy, Russ," she said. "Starr's a lucky woman. But I should get to bed. And you too. Thank you again."

"Don't mention it," he said.

I scrambled back into bed just moments before she came in. She crawled into bed very carefully, trying not to wake me. I was trying my hardest to swallow quietly; the anger had formed a lump in my throat that was making it hard to breathe. She was out in minutes, snoring softly. The smell of cigarette smoke clung to her clothes. She made me sick.

08

It was early when I woke up—I'd forgotten to close the blinds and sunlight was drilling beneath my eyelids—and for a minute I didn't remember what I'd overheard. Then that lump in my throat came back and I felt it again, that anger so strong I didn't know what to do with it. I put on the navy robe Starr had given me and wandered into the kitchen. As I was pouring milk on top of a heap of Corn Pops, Starr walked in. She wrapped one arm around my side like it was something people just did, and it felt good. "Eat quickly," she said. "We're getting out of the house today. You and me. It's my day off and I want to take you somewhere." I couldn't eat fast enough.

When I was done, I ran to my room and dressed, carelessly, but Starr wasn't ready when I walked into her bedroom. She was in the master bathroom, putting on makeup. "Come in if you want, Cal," she said. "I'm almost done." I walked in and sat on the lid of the toilet, hugging my knees to my chest.

Starr's silk robe gaped open, the sash slipping from the loop at her waist. She patted lotion onto her face, then fluttered her hands to help it sink in. Into her hands, she squeezed creamy tan foundation from a tube, then rubbed it into her forehead and cheeks, moving her hands outward and down until she'd covered her entire face. A faint line appeared on the side of her jaw, revealing the whiter skin of her neck. She twirled a poufy brush inside a compact of bronzer, then blew off the excess powder into the sink, speckling the porcelain. Sucking in her cheeks, she drew the brush up and under both cheekbones. She pulled out a pink and green tube of mascara from the giant makeup bag resting on the side of the sink, and leaned close to the mirror to apply it, opening her mouth involuntarily. The robe slipped open completely, and her breasts fell out, hanging down slightly as she leaned forward. "Sorry," she said, and laughed, but didn't stop putting on mascara to retie her robe. I stared. I wanted my body to look like Starr's. I wanted my tiny nipples to grow, wanted to wear a bra that had two separate cups you had to lean into, wanted to go to a tanning bed every other weekend like the older girls at my old school did, so that my whole body would be gleaming brown.

Starr twisted the cap back onto the mascara and retied her robe. I realized I'd been staring, and flushed, watching the redness spread across my face in the mirror like a flood. I shifted my gaze to myself. I hadn't looked at myself in the mirror like this since Starr had given me a haircut. Now my hair was stringy with grease. My tan had faded from being inside all the time. There was a pimple on my chin, probably from all the time I'd spent with my chin in my hands. I was too young and I was ugly.

Starr didn't say anything, though I knew she'd seen me looking at her body. She leaned forward again, sash double-knotted this time, and pulled her eyelid taut to draw a line in brown pencil just above her eyelashes. Russ had probably never seen her like this, I thought, turning herself into the version of Starr that she preferred. He'd seen her without makeup, but maybe I was the only one who had seen her in between.

Makeup was supposed to be like armor, but it was actually just as vulnerable as a bare face. When you wore makeup, you were showing everyone how you wished you really looked. You were admitting that you didn't look the way you wanted to. Somehow this just made me like Starr more.

I was only twelve. But already I knew I would never make myself that vulnerable. There was a connection between being vulnerable and being oblivious forming in my brain, like there was some direct link between every product Starr applied to her face and every night she went to bed early, unaware that Russ and her best friend from high school were staying up late on the couch, smoking and talking.

"Can I have some eyeliner?" I said, to break the silence.

"You don't need any," she said, smiling at me from the mirror. "Here," she said, pulling an aerosol can from beneath the sink. "Flip your head over." In that moment I would have done anything she'd asked. The spray was cool and powdery, and when she was done, she flipped me upright and sprayed my hairline as well. "There," she said, fluffing. "Now go wash your face and brush your teeth and you'll feel a million times better." She seemed steadier today than she normally was, like today she was the adult and I was the child, instead of us both falling somewhere in between. I ran to the other bathroom and did what she'd told me to. She was right, I did feel better.

When I got back to the bedroom, Starr was standing in front of the closet in her underwear. The floor was carpeted, and I didn't think she'd heard me come in. Like everything she owned, the bra and panties seemed to have been made for her, but decades ago; fitted to her body but old-fashioned in a way I loved but didn't understand.

My mom got our underwear from the drug store. Mine were white and boring. Starr's were lace and satin, and a peachy color that glowed next to her skin, the line where her underwear met her lower back giving me a feeling like envy and aching at the same time. A new feeling.

I had begun to catalogue new feelings and images, to store them away for the middle of the night when I couldn't sleep. This was one. How her silhouette went in and out, smallest in the middle; the way her bra rode up just slightly on her back. The wisps of hair grazing the back of her neck, escaping from the bun on top of her head, which I knew she would let down right before she left the house. It was for volume, she'd told a client once while I was reading on the living room couch next to the dryers. "Keep it up like this with a little hairspray and when you leave, shake it out. You'll have big hair all day."

I mimicked the way Starr was standing, leaning to one side and placing a hand on the middle of my back, elbow jutting out behind me. For someone who'd only worn robes since I met her, she had a lot of clothing. Everything looked fancy but faded, as if it had been hanging there undisturbed for months. Starr slid a dress off a hanger and slipped it over her head. "Zip me up?" she said. I pulled the zipper up slowly, keeping one hand at the edge of the seam to steady it. My hand brushed against her back as the zipper stopped. Her skin was as silky as her robes. She turned around. "Ready?" I nodded. I didn't know where we were going but I didn't care.

Starr's foot was heavy on the clutch, and we jerked back and forth as she navigated us out of the driveway. "Haven't done this in a long time!" she said. She was talking about driving but I was pretty sure she was also talking about leaving the house. Her car was clean and the seats were bleached from the sun. We didn't talk, but it felt like walking home from school with Shauna had been—a silence we could break at any time, but didn't need to.

We ended up in a park lining a river that Starr told me was the Willamette. I'd grown up minutes away from the ocean but I'd never been this close to the bank of a river before. She smoothed her dress down with one hand before sitting down on a wooden bench facing the river, and patted the spot beside her. "Your mom and I used to come here all the time in high school," she said. I tried to imagine a teenage version of my mom, older than me by just a few years, and couldn't. She had no pictures to show me. All I'd known of what she looked like was what I'd grown up with.

"Wasn't a far walk, and when we wanted to get away, we could come here. Used to be just us—until we got boyfriends, and then they'd bring us here together. But always together. Far as I know, neither of us came here alone. See that?" She pointed to a tall tree in a cluster surrounding a clearing, an X carved into its thick trunk. "That was our spot. Behind that tree. We had picnics there, we drank your grandmother's liquor there—I even lost my virginity behind that tree. I know that's not something you need to hear about now," she said, "but having you around feels—" she stopped. "It feels like we're what we used to be, me and your mom. Except it's you that feels like her, somehow." *Keep talking*, I thought. *Never stop talking.* "And your mother feels like a stranger," she said quietly.

She put her hand on mine. Her skin was smooth everywhere that I'd touched it so far. We watched the river without speaking until the sun was overhead, then she patted my hand and stood up.

The characters in her romance novels still seemed stupid to me but it didn't feel like they were being dramatic anymore.

Starr had gone to bed at nine. Now it was midnight, and we were still the only people in the house. I was in bed but wide awake, my hand vibrating from where she'd touched it earlier that afternoon. Starr in front of her closet, all lace and peach and tan. Starr's back, warm against the cool metal of the zipper.

Starr leaning over in front of the mirror, spilling out of the silk. Everywhere I'd touched, smooth.

The hand she'd touched went down the front of my underwear. I conjured up scenarios in which we could be together, each one more implausible than the next. Me feverish, her hand on my forehead, testing my temperature. Me in the bathtub, her walking in on me by mistake, then slipping out of her clothes and climbing in beside me. My fingers were slippery now, and my heart was pounding. I kept going, harder, eyes closed, Starr's naked body imprinted on my eyelids, faster, guided by the hand she'd touched until my back arched and my legs shook and my body fell still.

Immediately afterward I was mortified. It was as if she'd been in the room with me, as if my fantasies had been broadcast to everyone I'd ever known. In the bathroom, I scrubbed my hands under hot water until a film of soapy residue lined the sink. Flakes of soap had lodged themselves under my nails. It hurt, but I went back to bed like that anyway.

I woke to muffled conversation. The bedside clock, glowing red, told me it was 1:27 a.m. My mom and Russ were on the couch again, smoking again. "So I've got some good news," he said. "No warrant. Nothing. You're all clear."

"Oh, thank *god*," she said. "That's such a relief."

"Yep—you're good," he said.

"God, I just—left it all behind, for nothing. I mean, I was worried, but shit. What was I thinking?"

"It wasn't for nothing," Russ said. "Don't say that. You needed to go somewhere safe. Who knows what might have happened."

Daryl and my mom had been together for years. They fought but most of the time it was about how much my mom was drinking. Sometimes Daryl had slipped me twenty-dollar bills when he knew we were low on groceries. One of my book reports, red 'A+' scribbled on the front page, was hanging on his refrigerator.

"Me and Starr, we wanted to have kids real bad," he said. "Wasn't in the cards." My mom's voice was softer than his, but I could still hear her clearly. "Funny how it works out, isn't it," she said. "I never even wanted to have kids."

I didn't know what Russ was going to say to that. I didn't know what she meant, if she was happy to have me or not, if she was so drunk she was saying things she didn't mean or saying things she meant but was too afraid to say sober. I just knew I didn't want to hear any more. I put the pillow over my head and held it tight enough so I couldn't hear anything at all.

My mom and Russ talked every night now after Starr went to bed. And I was listening. I couldn't sleep if I knew they were out there. The more secrets I knew about somebody, the more powerful I felt. I didn't have anything else. So I listened. I learned we were headed back to Florida. Russ thought it was a good idea. "Just pay another month's rent on that place and move out," he said. "Callie should be back in school in the fall. You shouldn't have to hide."

"I can't afford that," she said.

"I'll cover it," he said. "Just enough to get you back and running. This place is full of waitresses—no wonder you couldn't find anything here. You know people back there. You'll make it work. Let me help you."

"I really can't let you do that," she said, in a way that suggested the only option she had was to let him.

"Jeanie, let me. We can afford it. Look, I'm just paying it forward. Someday you'll do it for someone else. Starr's always told me what a good person you were."

"Oh, but I'm not," she said. "I'm really not."

The first time she said it, it sounded like she was flirting but the second time it sounded like she really meant it.

Neither of them said anything for a long time. The light in the living room turned off—only the glow of the lamp by the couch was leaking into the hallway. I must have fallen asleep waiting for them to start talking again. When I woke up, my mom was beside me. On the bedside table, beneath an empty glass, was a check from Russell Evans. For a lot of money.

And then we were off. That same morning. "Oh, don't leave!" Starr said. "You know you can stay for as long as you want."

My mom gave her a strained smile. Russ was gone already. "It's okay," she said. "Gotta go back sometime. Can't let Callie think you can just run away from your problems."

"Listen," Starr said, in a lower voice. "I'd be happy to keep Callie here until you find a job. I wish I could give you some cash, but things are a bit tight right now. But letting her stay here for the rest of the summer wouldn't be a problem, if you want."

I wanted my mom to drive back without me. I wanted to stay with Starr and drink spritzers and sweep up hair from the living room floor and be with her all the time, instead of my mom. I wanted to tell her about my mom and Russell and the money, even though it would hurt her, because she deserved to know.

"I can handle my daughter, thanks," my mom said. Starr's face drooped underneath her makeup. "I'm sorry. I didn't mean it that way. I just—I can't imagine leaving without her. And you've already been so generous." She leaned in and hugged Starr tightly, then grabbed our bags and walked out the door.

Starr ran into the kitchen and came back with the navy silk robe I'd put in the laundry basket earlier that morning. "Take it with you," she said. "I gave it to you to keep. I'm going to miss you, sweetheart." She reached out and lifted my hair from my shoulders. "And condition those ends," she said, smiling, even though she still looked as if she were going to burst into tears. I felt like crying too, but I knew I wouldn't. It wouldn't solve anything.

I whispered goodbye, and wrapped my arms around her until I couldn't stand it anymore. She walked me to the door. Her mascara was running. My mom was already in the car. I climbed into the passenger seat but I didn't buckle my seatbelt.

I tried to picture the days ahead, what would happen when we pulled out of the driveway. Everything outside would begin to blur again and it would feel familiar, which made me intensely sad, that a blur was something I could get used to.

"I want to stay with Starr," I said softly. "You'd be happier that way." I knew it would hurt her, because a tiny bit of it was true.

"You don't know half the shit I've done for you," my mom said, "half the shit I've put up with to make sure you always get what you need. I'm not perfect. But I bend over backward for you."

"But I like it here." I was almost whispering by then.

"Starr doesn't actually *want* you to stay, Cal," she said, laughing. "You should know when people are just being polite." She exhaled deeply. We were still in the driveway, Starr watching us from the doorway in her pink silk, sunlight illuminating her messy morning hair. "You're stuck with me," she said. "And you're lucky. Someday you'll know."

09

We'd only been back from Oregon for a couple days, but we were picking up a moving truck the next morning to drive two hours northeast to Daytona, where my mom had found a job and an apartment through her friend Raelynn.

By now I knew not to ask for anything: saying goodbye to Shauna, or even giving her our new address, taking a last drive through the city I'd grown up in, the only place I'd ever known, ever even been, until we'd gone to Eugene. But just because I didn't ask didn't mean I didn't want it. My anger was simmering, tempered by being back home, even for only a little while.

The sky bruised purple and black out the living room window, lightning flashing through the darkness. The rain splattered on the windowpane, blowing sideways from the wind, and the cracks of thunder sent a jolt to my heart each time. I didn't realize how much I'd missed these summer storms, the ones where the sky sucked away the light so it was dark at 3 p.m., and the rain pelted your skin so hard it hurt.

It wasn't like we bought stuff all the time but we'd been in that apartment for a while and things just pile up, I guess. We were surrounded by boxes. My mom was moving fast, but she kept looking at the window when the storm started. We weren't talking much, unless it was to ask each other for the packing tape or something like that. I was learning how to leave places behind. I had already said goodbye to this place a thousand times in my head in Eugene—now I had to say goodbye to it again for good.

Just like that, the rain stopped, and the sky brightened again. The sun came back through the window, making patches of light on the floor. I started to sweat again, feeling it bead up on the back of my neck, underneath my hair, and on the small of my back. Ever since Starr had cut my hair I'd been wearing it down. It was still long but it looked good and I thought it made me look older.

I told my mom I was going for a last walk around the neighborhood. She didn't care. She was already a couple beers into a six-pack I hadn't even noticed her buy, taking a deep sip from a new bottle, the other one on the kitchen table, label peeled off in pieces and crumpled by its side.

It was humid and heavy and comforting outside—I hadn't known you could miss something as simple as air. Pink streaks were appearing behind the clouds, tearing holes in the cotton-candy sky, sun just beginning to set.

I did mean to just take a walk. I thought maybe I would sneak to a payphone and call Shauna, see if she could get her older brother to drive her by just so we could say goodbye. But I didn't know if she was upset with me for leaving without a word; if she'd even feel like being my friend anymore. So I didn't call Shauna. I walked to the corner of Howard and Mississippi and stuck out my thumb, like I was some runaway in a bad movie on TV late at night. A woman in a white station wagon pulled up alongside me, and I was thankful that she was old and that she wasn't a man. I wasn't stupid. She looked worried, but I told her

I was leaving a friend's house and my mom couldn't pick me up because her tire was flat. Then I gave her Daryl and Marcus's address.

I didn't know what I would have done if Daryl had been outside, if he'd been home at all. But I didn't have to worry about that because Marcus was working out on his machines when I got there. He almost dropped the bench press on his chest when I called out his name.

"Cal? What the hell are you doing here?"

I'd already used up my boldness for the day, hitchhiking with that woman. "We left and I didn't think we'd come back but then we came back but now we're leaving again and my mom doesn't want Daryl to know we came back so don't tell but I just wanted to say goodbye and—" It all came out in a rush.

"He's playing a gig tonight," Marcus said. "You got lucky. You just missed him."

I smiled with one side of my mouth. "That's good, I guess."

"You're fucking right it is. God, Daryl was so mad at your mom. Where did you take off to, anyway? He parked outside your apartment for days. Cost him a shit ton of money to get that car fixed, you know." I shrank.

"Fuck, I'm sorry," Marcus said. "It's not your fault. It's not your fault at all. I'm an ass. That's between your mom and Daryl."

"Yeah, well," I said. I wanted him to invite me in. I wanted to tell him that I knew how to make a spritzer now, that I knew how to drink. "She's kinda crazy." It felt like a betrayal but also like a relief, saying that.

Marcus laughed and shook his head. "You're damn right about that. It's a wonder you turned out like you did." The sky was burning purple and orange now. I was still just standing there, wondering how long it would take before my mom wondered where I was. If she would even notice.

He wasn't making any move to invite me in so I asked him if we could go up to the roof of the trailer. "You know, like when you showed me the stars?" I pulled at the threads hanging from the ends of my cutoffs.

Marcus pulled up his tank top to wipe his face, and I saw a line of dark hair running from his belly button down into his shorts. It made me blush and I hoped he hadn't seen it. I hitched up the strap of my bra from where it had started to slip. I'd started wearing real bras, not training bras, most of the time now. I didn't really need them, I guess, but I liked the slippery feel on my skin, liked the faint black shadow that showed under my t-shirts. I thought it made me look grown up. I knew my bra was showing through the white tank top I'd been wearing to pack up the apartment.

"Sure," Marcus said, shrugging, and stood up. He took my hand and I felt like I did when Starr had rested her hand on mine. "Climb on up."

We settled down on the roof. I stretched my legs out in front of me, hoping Marcus would notice how long they'd gotten, even though I was pale from missing a month of Florida summer and spending every day inside. I leaned back, sticking my chest out a bit. The sun had set completely by then, without me even noticing. "So, any constellations to show me tonight?" I said, and looked over at him.

He smiled. "You can't get off that easy, Calliope. I want to know why you're here." I hadn't even known he knew my real name. Every other person called me Cal or Callie. I raised my eyebrows. "What? I love that name," he said. "You know what Calliope means, don't you?"

"I dunno. Yeah," I said. I had no idea. Marcus smiled like he knew I didn't.

"*The muse of epic poetry*," he said. "It's Greek. Daughter of Zeus. Like every other woman in Greek mythology. Well, daughter or lover, I guess." He laughed. It would take years before I understood what he meant. "Where the hell did Jeanie come up with Calliope? Anyway, you know what a muse is?" I shook my head.

"An inspiration. Someone who gives other people ideas. But the thing about Calliope is, she wasn't just a muse. All the ancient pictures of her have her writing. She had her own ideas too. And that's who you are, Calliope. Other people feed off of you, you know that? But you have your own ideas."

Marcus knew so much more than I did. Than most adults did. Or maybe what he knew was just more interesting than whatever anybody else talked about.

"So. Where the fuck did you and Jeanie take off to?" he asked.

"Oregon," I said. "We were gonna stay with my grandma but she was dead so we stayed with my mom's friend from high school instead. But we're not staying in Tampa. We're moving to Daytona tomorrow."

Marcus shook his head. "Your mom is a piece of work," he said. "Let me take you home. She's got to be worried about you by now." I shrugged.

"Hey, can I tell you something?" he said. "I missed having you around. Ah, I don't know what I'm saying. I spent the whole summer just working and working out. Broke up with Kelly. Spent a couple nights on this roof, actually, by accident. Fell asleep up here. Lucky I didn't fall off. I thought about you guys the whole time. I was so worried about you. You know Daryl even went to your school? To see if they knew anything? God! Jeanie needs to know, if nothing else, that she can't do this shit to you. It's not fair." I'd felt selfish even thinking that. But when Marcus said it, I felt better, like maybe I actually had something to be upset about.

"I know. It was a pretty shitty summer," I said. I was still thinking about Kelly. I couldn't tell if I hadn't liked her or if I'd just been jealous of her. The last time I'd seen her she'd been wearing those glittery butterfly clips from Circle K, which I thought was a little weird, like, that was something *I* should have been wearing, not Marcus's girlfriend.

"Apparently Oregon taught you some bad words," Marcus said, grinning. He lay down with his hands underneath his head, elbows sticking out to the side. "What'd you get up to in Oregon, anyway? You all corrupted now, Cal?"

"No," I said. "I just drank, mostly."

"Ah, fuck," Marcus said. "How old are you anyway, Cal? Thirteen?"

"Twelve," I mumbled.

"You shouldn't be drinking at twelve!" he said. "Jesus. Who the fuck gave you alcohol?"

"My mom's friend," I said quietly. "But it was okay. It was during the day and we were just at her house. I didn't, you know, actually get really drunk or anything." I thought Marcus would think I was cool but now I was just embarrassed. I'd said the wrong thing.

"It's not your fault," Marcus said. "You're young." Everyone kept telling me that, but at that moment it felt like an insult, something blatantly untrue. Every day I was changing. I was shooting upward, shedding my skin, letting my hair grow long and silky down my back.

I was obsessed with the feel of things, touching everything, because lately it seemed like I was saying goodbye faster than I could keep up with. It was all I could do to drag my hand along the bumpy walls of the apartment, rest my head against the cool tile of the kitchen floor while I was supposed to be cleaning so we could get our security deposit back.

The last few days in the apartment had been unbearably hot—the power had been turned off while we were gone, and it didn't make sense to go through the process of setting it back up when we were just leaving again. We slept on top of the sheets, windows open and cheap drugstore fans swirling the tepid air around us. I wore the robe Starr had given me, and nothing else, waking up sweaty and disoriented, clutching for the heavy comforter on the guest bed at Starr's before I realized where I was. I'd dreamed about her almost every night since we'd left.

"It's not a bad thing, being young," Marcus said, and I tuned back in, flushed from the memory of my dream from the night before. I wanted to be touched, held, feel someone else's skin on my own. I didn't know then exactly what desire was. I just didn't want to be lonely. I just wanted someone to touch me for a little while.

I put my hand on his arm, just like Starr had done to my hand. Before he could move, I rolled on top of him, positioning my legs directly on top of his, bending my arms to match his. From above, we must have looked like those body outlines Shauna and I used to draw around each other in chalk on the basketball court during recess—loose, larger versions of our own bodies. For a second, I felt as if I could fall asleep with my head on his chest, using his warm body like a mattress. I wanted to explode with happiness.

Marcus sat up immediately, pushing me off. Not roughly, but forcefully. "Jesus, Cal!" he said. He looked incredibly sad. "Do you know how old I am?" I didn't. I had no clue. I didn't even think what I'd done was wrong. I was aching for someone. I wanted to be wanted. I didn't yet know in what way.

I started to cry. "I'm sorry," I said, wiping my tears away with the back of my hand. "I didn't, I don't know." I looked off in the opposite direction, above the roofs of the rest of the trailer park, toward the interstate that stretched across the sky. "I just want someone to touch me," I said. "Not like, you know. Just someone to hold me." I still couldn't look at him.

I wanted him to touch me and I wanted to touch all the bodies I'd ever known, wanted to be back in bed when my mom came in early in the morning to spoon me, to be nestled in between my old babysitter and her boyfriend on the couch, to be back in the shower with Shauna in our bathing suits, bumping into each other as we both tried to stand underneath the stream of hot water to rinse the chlorine out of our hair. To be back in Eugene, looking out at the Willamette River with Starr's hand on mine. I was so, so lonely.

"It's just not fair!" I said, more intensely than I'd meant to.

"You're right," Marcus said. "It's not. And that's just how it is when you get older. You're learning. You gotta rise above it." I had no idea how you were supposed to do that, but I just nodded, and hugged my knees to my chest.

"Oh, c'mere," he said, and scooted closer to me, looping his arm around my body. I leaned my head on his shoulder and closed my eyes. He let me stay like that for I don't know how long. Marcus was a good person. Just another good person I had to leave behind.

He took me home on the bus—we sat next to each other in silence the whole way. "You mean a lot to so many people, Callie," he said. "Just because you leave someone behind doesn't mean they forget about you." He hugged me and got up at the stop before mine so my mom wouldn't see him. "Bye, Calliope," he called out from the front of the bus. The mechanical doors swung back into place, and the bus lurched forward. My right shoulder smelled like his deodorant from when he'd held me on the roof.

I was sad when I got back to the apartment, but I wasn't angry anymore. My mom didn't even ask why I'd stayed out so long, or what I'd been doing. She was finishing another beer and packing up the last of our kitchen stuff, wrapping the big flowery plates in newsprint from the stack of local papers she'd grabbed from the newspaper rack at the drugstore a few blocks away. I hoped maybe she'd start cooking again sometime in our new apartment. We usually ate restaurant leftovers but on her days off we used to have taco night and big pots of spaghetti and even pork chops sometimes. I liked cooking with her beside me, helping me. But we were both different now. We were both older. I could cook by myself.

She didn't look up when I came in, just put her thighs on either side of the box to push it closed and started to tape it shut, filling the apartment with the awful sound of tape peeling off of itself. "Next is your bed," she said. "We can sleep on the mattresses tonight. Just one less thing to do tomorrow morning. Go see if you can get started. Tools are over there."

It wasn't as hot sleeping on the floor that night, maybe because of the storm from earlier, and I slept underneath the sheets. I couldn't remember any of my dreams when I woke up.

10

I first saw Jazz in the parking lot of our new apartment complex, unloading groceries with her mom. She was wearing a bikini top and denim cutoffs and I was jealous because I just had a couple of old one-pieces, faded from chlorine and saltwater. We just stared at each other that time. But we were the only girls our age in the building, and by the end of the week we were best friends. All the old ladies called us "those girls," and everyone knew who they were talking about. We looked alike, same blond hair and brown eyes, and we liked it. We tried to convince everyone we met we were twins, even though Jazz was a year older, thirteen, which sounded much older than twelve.

By the end of the summer, the temperature had hit 99 in Daytona Beach. Jazz got her period for the first time. We met Johnny.

Jazz would come by every morning after my mom left for work, her flip-flops slapping the concrete walkway as she approached. She'd help me fold up the pullout couch in the living room where I slept. Then we'd stand in front of the narrow mirror by the kitchenette, holding our arms against each other to see who'd gotten darker. Jazz had a picture of Christie Brinkley that she'd torn out of a *Sports Illustrated* at the drugstore. "I want to look like this by the end of the summer," she'd said.

She was perfecting the art of liquid eyeliner, and I'd watch in the mirror as she tried to keep her hand steady, whispering *fuck* when she slipped up, and licking her pointer finger to wipe the mistakes away. Then she'd practice on me. Later, dark streaks would trickle down the sides of our faces as we tanned on the beach, eyes closed to the afternoon sun.

After doing our makeup, we'd grab towels and flounce downstairs, armed with baby oil and the sunglasses Jazz had stolen for us from the drugstore. I'd watched her do it. She ripped off the tags and stuck the sunglasses in her hair. She even winked at the cashier on our way out, a pimply boy who went to the high school on North Oleander. Jazz would do anything if you dared her to. Sometimes she dared herself if nobody else was around.

The day Jazz and I met Johnny I'd been putting off doing laundry until I ran out of everything, so she helped me carry a crusty pile of clothes that smelled of mildew and Hawaiian Tropic to the laundromat. With the extra quarters, we bought bubble gum from the machine outside and filled our mouths with large gobs that hurt to chew. Then we sat on the plastic chairs, sweaty and sticky, and blew bubbles as we watched the laundry turn. Jazz stood next to me while I folded, one pile of my mom's clothes and another pile of mine.

We'd only been on the beach for a little while that afternoon when Jazz decided we should give up on tanning. The heat was damp and piercing; you felt as if you would fry if you stayed in the same position for too long. Instead, we walked ankle-deep along the shallows toward the Holiday Inn. There was a snack bar there on the beach, and when this one guy was working there, Jazz could usually get us something for free.

We were halfway down the beach when Jazz got bored. "I dare you to ask him for a beer," she said, and tilted her head toward a potbellied man sitting on a faded towel next to a sweating cooler. I shook my head. "Fine then," she said. "I'll do it, if you're gonna be a baby."

"Hi sir," Jazz said. The man looked up and slid off his sunglasses. She leaned over to him real slow, and whispered something in his ear. He scratched his head, then reached into the cooler and handed her a Miller Lite, flipping off the top with his lighter. Jazz smiled sweetly at him and darted back to me, flushed and giddy. "See how easy it is?" she said, as if she almost couldn't believe it herself. She offered me a sip and even though I didn't like beer, I took a swig.

Jazz tossed the empty beer bottle into the ocean when we got to the snack bar. I watched it bob on the surface for a minute, then gather water and sink with the next wave. "Is Derek working today?" she asked the lady behind the counter.

The lady raised her eyebrows. "No, sweetie. But I'll tell him some girls came looking for him. You know you're not allowed to sit here unless you buy something." Derek always let us sit there without buying anything. I felt like he would have preferred it if Jazz showed up alone, but she always brought me along. The woman turned to the guy sitting next to us.

"Now what can I get you, sir?"

"I'll take a Corona if you've got one, and, what the heck, two virgin daiquiris for those two." He turned toward us and stood up. "Unless you'd rather have piña coladas? I'm Johnny, by the way." His shoulders were broad and reddened, and when he moved his arm to reach for his wallet, I could see the muscles twitch beneath his skin. He was the kind of guy that looked cute from far away but up close when you saw him in sharper focus he didn't seem that special. Jazz arched her back slightly. I noticed grey clouds forming above us, and the temperature dropping a bit.

"Hi Johnny," Jazz said, in that voice she used to talk to men we didn't know. "I'm Jazz and this is Callie. We're twins."

Jazz slipped onto the stool next to Johnny's and propped her bony elbows on the counter while she sipped her daiquiri. She swiveled back and forth slowly on the seat. We couldn't touch the floor from the stools, and our feet swung in the air. She'd only been talking to him for a few minutes when the sky rumbled so loudly the counter shook for a second.

"Looks like the sky's about to open up," Johnny said. "Tell you what—I'm gonna head back up to my place. Why don't you two come over, watch some television, wait out the storm?" It was about to pour. And we were pretty far from our building. But this would be the biggest dare I'd seen Jazz accept yet. I started to say something, but she grabbed my hand and squeezed it hard.

"We'll come," she said.

Johnny's building looked just like ours, and it made me feel better, as if somehow we knew him already. As if we'd been there before. There were the same stucco walls, the mosquitoes gathered in the stairwell, the sandy welcome mats in the hall. "After you," he said when we got to his door, and we stepped inside. He kept his apartment really cold.

Jazz and I sat down on the couch, our bare thighs sticking to the leather. Johnny took a seat on the armchair next to us. Up close, the skin on his face was bumpy, and he had angry dots on his cheeks, from shaving maybe, or picking at things he should have left alone. He was both old and ageless, in the way that all adults are until you become one yourself. He could have been twenty or forty.

"So what do you girls like to do for fun?" Johnny said. "You certainly seem to spend a lot of time in the sun... both of you have gorgeous tans, y'know. Both of y'all are real cute."

Jazz smiled. "We don't do much else during the summer. I don't want to go back to school."

"Yeah, school. That's a bummer. Are you two at Seabreeze?"

Jazz blurted out, "No, Hinson Junior," before I could stop her, and I bit my lip. But Johnny didn't seem to care that we weren't even in high school. He just laughed and said *Hoo boy* under his breath.

"Do you go to school, Johnny?" Jazz said.

"Nah," he said. "I'm in construction. Working on one of those new high rises way up on Ocean Shore right now."

"Oh." Jazz sounded impressed, or maybe intimidated, because she didn't say anything back. We were all quiet for a moment. I didn't know what else to talk about. He turned to us, looked us up and down like he was trying to memorize our bodies. I couldn't move. Jazz wasn't doing anything and if Jazz still thought we were okay, then I had to think so too.

Jazz slapped her hand on her thigh and I jumped. "Mosquito," she said, wiping it off on the arm of the couch. "Um, actually, where's your bathroom?"

"Here, I'll show you," Johnny said, and stood up. He put his hand on the small of her back to direct her. "It's that door on the left there." Even though it wasn't me he'd touched I got goose bumps. Johnny sat back down, this time next to me. The cushion sank under his weight, and I leaned to the left to stop myself from sliding toward him. "So, uh, you two are twins? Fraternal, I guess. That's cool."

"Well, Jazz likes to say that," I said real soft, picking at my cuticles. "But we're just best friends. Not twins."

Johnny laughed. "So you're not twins. Anything else you two are lying about?" He raised an eyebrow. "It's not nice to lie, you know." Jazz would have known what to say back, how to play along, but all I could do was nod. "Aw, I'm just kidding," he said. Then he reached out and stroked the top of my right thigh, tracing a circle with his thumb. My tan went white under the pressure of his finger. I bit my tongue. We heard the toilet flush. And then I did something bad. I slipped out from under Johnny's hand and I ran for the door.

Johnny called out, "Callie! Wait!" and started to follow me, but he stopped when the bathroom door opened. So did I, but only for a second. Somehow I knew he wouldn't chase me, not with Jazz still there. I ran to the end of the hallway, and in the staircase I bent over the railing, heaving. I felt like throwing up but nothing would come out. I walked barefoot along the beach back to my apartment, following the receding line of the tide. It wasn't even dark yet. I turned my head each time I saw a girl out of the corner of my eye, but none of them was Jazz.

When my mom came home from the restaurant that night, I was still up, watching reruns of *Love Connection*, holding the phone in my hand and dialing the first six digits of Jazz's phone number over and over, then chickening out. She flopped onto the couch and peeled money from her pocket, sorting ones and fives, humming along to the *Love Connection* theme song. "God, Callie, I'm dying for a cigarette. Come downstairs with me?" I didn't want to be alone, so I followed her to the parking lot. We sat on the hood of our car, the night air like a warm blanket, and I breathed in the smoke on purpose until it made my lungs raw.

As soon as we got back upstairs, my mom passed out on the couch. I put a blanket over her as she snored softly, then curled up in her bed in the bedroom and fell asleep.

My body was warm and achy when I woke up. I went to the bathroom to pee and in the mirror I was bright red. "Ooh, that burn looks bad. Maybe you should stay inside today," my mom said on her way out the door. "You and Jazz can paint each other's nails or something. I think there's aloe vera in the bathroom cabinet." The skin on my back and shoulders peeled off in lazy strips for days. I wondered if Jazz had gotten burned too.

I only saw Jazz one more time after that, a few months later. She'd started high school that year, but I was still stuck in junior high, so we didn't even take the same bus in the mornings. I walked out to the parking lot to grab a cassette from the car, and there she was. She had dark circles under her eyes and she looked older, like she could pass for seventeen or eighteen. Jazz spoke first. "We're moving," she said, and lifted a suitcase into the trunk. "My mom's got a boyfriend now and they're pretty serious. She met him at Caribbean Jack's, but he's from Texas. He's rich. We should have left two hours ago. We're running late."

I hooked my thumbs into the belt loops of my shorts. "Jazz," I said, but that was all that came out. I meant to say a lot of other things, but I didn't know how. "Well, write me if you want," I said instead.

She smiled without opening her mouth, and shrugged her shoulders. "Yeah, I guess," she said, and climbed into the passenger side. Her mom shifted clumsily, and the car jerked into reverse. I watched them wait at the stop sign, then turn onto South Atlantic and speed away. I stood there for a long time, in the parking lot of the Bella Vista, until the heat from the asphalt started to burn the soles of my feet.

11

I didn't spend much time alone at the beach after what happened with Johnny. I kept thinking I might run into him, which scared me. But it also excited me a little bit in a way that I didn't like to think about, a way that made me feel like a bad person. So I went to the community pool instead. It was crowded and noisy in the afternoons, but if I got there early in the morning, it was mostly old people swimming laps, and I had a few hours of quiet before the whole neighborhood showed up.

I usually changed into my swimsuit before I came to the pool. I hated the feeling of taking off my clothes in open spaces, and in front of other people, especially people I didn't know. But there was something about that locker room in particular that was calming. It wasn't like the one at school, bright and grimy at the same time, all shouts and laughter and metallic clangs. It was damp and cool in this locker room, and the walls were covered in navy tile so it was always dark. I liked being around the women at the pool more than the girls I went to school with. The old women changed slowly, almost leisurely. They were comfortable, not fixated on their bodies the way I was. Not ashamed.

I was constantly, constantly aware of my own body. The prickles on my legs when I hadn't shaved them for a few days. The pinched skin at my armpits that folded over the sides of my strapless dresses. The sweat that formed on the undersides of my thighs when I sat at the outdoor tables at the Oasis, or the leather seats of the school bus. The way my left breast felt heftier, more substantial than my right one when I cupped them both in my hands. The wetness in my underwear that came on sudden and concentrated, unexpected.

I remembered how Jazz had asked me, in a rare moment when she wasn't pretending she knew more about growing up than I did, if it was normal to find white stuff in your underwear sometimes. We were watching TV, and she'd just come back from the bathroom. "Cal?" she said, biting her lip before she asked me. "Does this ever happen to you?" I had been wondering the same thing. I wanted to cry with relief. Nobody had taught us anything about becoming women. We were figuring it out on our own.

I wasn't looking at the women in the locker room in a creepy way. I just liked to reassure myself that there were so many ways to be normal. A body didn't need to be so complicated.

I chose a locker and threw my flip-flops in, tossing my cutoffs and tank top inside. I was wearing my mom's black string bikini because I liked the way the top looked on me, even though I obsessively tied and retied the strings on the bottoms because I was terrified they'd fall off. I brought my sunglasses, towel, and an issue of *Cosmopolitan* out to the deck. I'd found the magazine the last time I was at the pool, wavy and crinkled from sitting in a shallow puddle of pool water. My mom didn't care what I read, but she never bought magazines. They were a waste of money.

Sometimes we stood in the magazine aisle at the grocery store, my mom flipping idly through a magazine while I absorbed every tidbit of information inside as if there would be a test on the contents later on. After a while, they all started to sound the same, but in a comforting way. Like there were formulas to being a woman, and you just needed to be reminded every so often of the right ways to act, the right things to say, the right clothes to wear.

I found a deck chair with all the vinyl strips intact and spread my towel over it, wincing slightly at the heat coming off of the salmon-colored concrete that made the bottoms of my bare feet prickle with pain. I liked to lay out until I got so hot I felt like I would faint, until sweat soaked my hairline and trickled down the center of my chest. Then I'd jump straight into the deep end. It felt better that way, when I'd denied myself of something for as long as I could stand it before giving in.

I watched the old people paddling, slipping underneath the water then surfacing again, pushing off at the edge to head back in the opposite direction. One woman clung to the side, goggles around her neck, catching her breath. Her skin was a deep roasted brown, mottled and folded in on itself like a crumpled piece of paper. I'd seen her in the locker room before, stretching out her swim cap before tugging it on. I didn't understand the appeal of swimming laps. Nor the appeal of running on a treadmill, which was something my mom constantly talked about wanting. When she was home and we stayed up watching TV late enough, a certain infomercial came on—a woman who wasn't sweating at all, who wore white bike shorts and a pink leotard, thick white ankle socks and bright new tennis shoes. She walked briskly along the moving belt, telling the camera how exciting it was. But it didn't get you anywhere. When you were done, you were just back in the same place you'd started out. It was as if you hadn't done anything at all.

I stood up, sweaty and sunbaked, ready to immerse myself. My back had been hurting all morning, a dull ache low down, and I was looking forward to the strange but comforting feeling of being held together by water, liquid pressing my body together, keeping it intact.

But something felt weird, like I'd been walking down stairs and missed a step—that sensation of hurtling into air, your stomach dropping. I felt sticky, not from sweat. I was opening up.

I sat in one of the bathroom stalls with my swimsuit bottoms down, scrubbing at the crotch of my bathing suit with a damp piece of toilet paper that was crumbling in my hand. I'd never been more grateful for an empty locker room than I was now. No one had seen me rush out of the bathroom stall, fumble for quarters in my bag, retrieve a tampon from the vending machine mounted to the wall. No one had heard me whispering the directions from the paper insert inside the box, as if it would make more sense if I read it aloud.

It was no use. There was still a faded but persistent brownish-red spot on the bathing suit bottoms I'd borrowed from my mom. I would have to tell her. I pulled them back on again, still damp, and got dressed, smoothing my hand over the back of my butt several times to make sure I hadn't bled through my shorts, a gesture that would become almost automatic to me.

On my walk home, I tried to figure out how I would tell my mother. I thought maybe she'd be happy, even though I'd ruined her bathing suit.

For a brief second I forgot about everything, envisioned calling Jazz when I got home, telling her gleefully that we were on the same side of the divide again.

12

"You know, you're really getting on my nerves," my mom said one night when she got home from work. She hadn't even closed the door yet. I sat up, turned the volume on the TV down.

"You're always here, just reading or watching TV. Don't you want to *do* something? Don't you have any friends?" It was going to be a mean night. These were happening more and more often now. "I get home from work every night and I just want to be alone sometimes, you know? No offense, but I'm around a bunch of shitheads for hours and when I get home I want to *relax*. This apartment's small, I know. But Jesus, Cal, you haven't had any friends since Jazz moved, what, two years ago? I don't know what went on between the two of you anyway." I started to say something, but she held up her hand. "Honestly, I don't care.

"The point is, you need something to do—*not* in this apartment. If you're not going to go make any friends, I'm going to find you a job. There's a couple that came in with a baby the other day… not your typical Oasis customers." She laughed. "I mean, they're rich as shit. I can tell just from her wedding ring. What a rock.

"Babies are easy, as long as you can give 'em back at the end of the night." She stared at me, like it was my fault I'd been a baby once, my fault she couldn't have handed me over to anyone else.

"I don't have a bedroom," I said, not in a mean way. It was just true. "That's why I have to be in the living room when you get home. This *is* my bedroom."

"I'm doing *all* I can for you. All by myself. You have no idea." She looked disgusted. She unhooked her bra from underneath the Oasis polo shirt, pulled it out from one sleeve, dropped it on the floor. "Why don't you go take a walk? Go out on the beach. We live a street away from the fucking *ocean*. My god, take advantage of it!"

I slipped on some flip-flops and walked out, letting the screen door slam behind me. I didn't go to the ocean. I walked to the other side of the complex, along the catwalk that connected all of the buildings, until I reached Jazz's old apartment. The welcome mat outside the door was new, and the sandy shoes outside the door were children's shoes, bright and tiny. I knew she didn't live there anymore. But I didn't know where else to go. I slumped down in the darkness, leaning against the railing across from her old apartment. A tiny dark thought wound its way into my head until I could barely breathe. She was right. I didn't have anyone. Except for her.

"Here's the number of the house we'll be at, and here are the neighbors' numbers—don't hesitate to call!" Mrs. Silverman pointed out a paper on the fridge. "So glad you could make it," she said. "Our regular babysitter had a date tonight, and I just didn't know how we were going to make it to this benefit!" She smiled again. "Callie, right? Your mother's told me so much about you—she's so proud of your grades!" She'd never told me that before. "And you've already taken a class in child CPR—my goodness, you're quite motivated."

I swallowed. I had no idea what child CPR even was. What

else had my mother told her? "Yep!" I said, and smiled. "Where *is* Max?" I asked.

"Oh, he's asleep already!" she said. "No nap today—he was out like a light. He shouldn't even wake up, but if he does, you can let him cry for a minute before you go in. He usually calms himself down. There's formula on the counter, and a bottle right here. You can give him that if he really won't fall back asleep." She hadn't stopped moving since I'd arrived, pointing out the fridge, and the pantry, where I could help myself, and the television, and the spiral staircase that led up to the bedrooms, where Max was sleeping. "Steve—Mr. Silverman—is already in the car," she said. "We're running late, as always. Just have a good night! We should be home around midnight." She locked the door from the outside when she left. I watched through the frosted glass as her blurry silhouette moved across the yard and climbed into the car. I was alone.

I had no interest in watching TV, no matter how big or fancy the screen was, no matter how many videotapes they had in the big wooden cabinet underneath the television. The TV was constantly on at our apartment, and most of the time I wasn't even watching. My mom liked to watch TV, but even when she wasn't there sometimes I changed the channel to a sitcom or a soap opera, and went into her room to read or stare up at the ceiling, pretending there were people just in the other room, having a conversation, that I wasn't completely alone.

I was hungry. I ran my hand along the slab of marble on top of the island in the middle of the kitchen. It was cool under my hand, and felt heavy and expensive. It was light pink, flecked with grey, and I wondered if Mr. Silverman had wanted a pink countertop. I felt like it was Mrs. Silverman's decision. I felt like Mrs. Silverman probably got her way a lot.

The refrigerator was full, but instead of tinfoil and beer and takeout containers, there was fresh fruit, cold cuts, leftovers stacked neatly in Tupperware. Baby food lined up in jars. In the freezer, there were three flavors of Häagen-Dazs ice cream. I opened all of them. Someone had used an actual ice cream scoop, not just a spoon.

I took out some spaghetti and meatballs from the back of the fridge, and ate it straight from the container, using a polished silver fork that I was pretty sure was only for special occasions. I meant to stop before it was obvious that I'd eaten any, but before I knew it I was twirling the last of the pasta onto my fork. *Shit.* She'd said to eat anything but I didn't know if she'd really meant it. Sometimes people said a lot of things they didn't mean, just to be polite. I washed and dried the Tupperware and hid it in the back of a cabinet, hoping she wouldn't notice I'd taken anything from the fridge. Then I wiped my hands on my shorts and walked upstairs.

The Silvermans' bedroom was huge, and the floor was covered in a white carpet that looked so soft and clean I took off my shoes before walking on it. I felt dirty and out of place in my denim cutoffs and tank top, like I should be wearing something fancy. Everything was white—the sheets, the carpet, the furniture, the pillows. There was a bathtub that looked like a Jacuzzi and two sinks side by side in the bathroom. I wondered if Mr. and Mrs. Silverman brushed their teeth next to each other, if she did her makeup in the mornings while he shaved off his stubble. He probably had a job where you had to shave every morning.

I wandered into the closet—one you could walk into—and ran my hand over the shoulders of the identical blue button-downs on Mr. Silverman's side of the closet. Stroked his ties. I didn't know what he did for work but it was obviously something important. He was definitely in charge of something. I moved over to Mrs. Silverman's side, studying the dresses and pantsuits. I wondered if I would ever have a job where I had to wear a pantsuit. The hangers were coated with velvet.

I had reached an age where my teachers had started to tell us that we could be anything. "If you try hard enough, you can be anything you want to be!" read a poster in Mr. Gomez's classroom. But I wanted to be someone else completely. There was no way to try hard enough for that.

I slid one of the dresses off of its hanger. Black and beaded, with thin straps and a back that dipped low. It was a little big on me, but Mrs. Silverman was small, and it stayed on my shoulders. The weight of it surprised me. I slid a pair of silver heels out from a cubbyhole. She was a seven, just like me. I pulled my hair up and puffed it with one hand, trying to make it look like the fluffy hair all the girls had in magazines. I stared at myself in the full-length mirror, twirling around to see my ass, which was sticking out more than usual because of the heels. I admired my back in the mirror, how the dress dipped low, lower than the waistline of my cutoffs, which were in a pile with my tank top on the floor.

I almost felt like I was someone else, like I had tried hard enough. Only my eyes betrayed me—reminding me that I was just looking back at myself. I wasn't someone new. I would never be Mrs. Silverman, or anyone like Mrs. Silverman. I wanted to rip that poster off the wall of the classroom. I wanted to ask Mr. Gomez if he had tried hard enough, if that was the 'anything' he had wanted to be. I wanted to tell my mom she hadn't tried hard enough—that maybe if she had, I *could* be something. But I knew that would make her sad or angry. And I didn't want that, didn't want to make anyone feel the way I had the other night when I'd walked to Jazz's old apartment.

My arm hurt from holding up my hair, and I let it down, unzipping the dress and letting it slip to the floor. I felt a tiny thrill from being naked in someone else's house. I hung up the dress and put the shoes back exactly as they'd been.

Mrs. Silverman had so many pairs of underwear, and bras to match. I wondered what it was like to get undressed in front of someone, to put yourself on display like that. I found a small purple bra in the back of a dresser drawer, with mesh cups that you could see right through, and a pair of underwear to match, purple mesh with purple flowers embroidered on the sides. I put them on. I wanted someone to undress me, to be surprised at what was underneath. I wanted to show Marcus, or Starr, someone who thought I was just a kid still. I wasn't a kid anymore. I was fourteen.

I could get used to wearing underwear like this, I thought. *I would like to get dressed every morning in a closet like this.*

Max let out a couple of soft cries, and I startled, stripping in a hurry, and putting my own clothes back on. I stuck the bra and underwear in my pocket. Mrs. Silverman had everything. I could have that.

I tiptoed into his room, but he was already asleep again, and I just stood over the crib, watching his little baby chest rise and fall. I kind of wished I'd gotten there when he was still awake. I wanted to know if he was heavy to hold. I couldn't believe how tiny his fingers were, his fingernails. I reached in and put my pointer finger on his palm. In his sleep, he curled his hand around my finger, more strongly than I'd expected. He wouldn't remember this, and that made me feel powerful and sad at the same time. I wondered how many things I didn't remember, if I would want to remember them. I wondered if my mom had snuck into my room when I was little, just to watch my fingers curl around hers. I didn't even know if I'd had a room of my own.

There are just a few pictures of me as a baby. In one of them, I'm slumped over my mom's shoulder, pouty and asleep. She looks beautiful, but exhausted. The circles under her eyes stick out even in the photo, making her eyes look bigger than normal. Almost like she's pleading for help. I don't know who took the picture. My mom always says she doesn't remember.

I heard a noise downstairs and froze. They weren't supposed to be home for another hour at least. I clung to the side of the crib. I wasn't sure if I should go look, stay here with the baby, or grab him and hide. But he'd wake up if I did that. I was shaking when I heard "Callie?" coming lightly from downstairs. It was Mrs. Silverman. I walked out of the baby's room to find her coming up the stairs. Her bangs were flopping onto her forehead now, and her lipstick had faded and creased into the corners of her mouth. She was holding her heels in one hand and the corner of her dress in another. She still looked beautiful but she looked tired, and confused.

"What were you doing upstairs? Is Max all right?" she asked, and breezed by me, leaving a faint and temporary scent of perfume that had been too strong at the beginning of the night. Before I could answer, she came out and flopped down on the top of the staircase, her dress billowing out behind her. "God, I thought something had happened when I couldn't find you, and then you were up with the baby…" she was talking to herself more than me. I sat down next to her, my denim cutoffs riding up, thighs flattening, goose bumps spreading down my legs from how cold they kept the house.

"I was just making sure he was okay," I said. "I mean, I didn't want anything to happen while you were gone. Sorry."

She laughed. "Don't be sorry! I'm glad you care. I must have scared you, coming home early. I just missed him."

"But he's asleep," I said, feeling dumb.

"Oh, I know," she said. "I'm not going to wake him up or anything. I just... it's embarrassing. I hate to be away from him for too long. Even Steve—my husband—thinks I'm silly. But he'll catch a ride home later. I had to see my little Max. I can't stop thinking about him when I'm not with him." She sighed, in a happy way. "Did you have dinner?"

I nodded. "Thanks. It was good." It had been really good. There was so much in their fridge.

"Is your mother able to pick you up?" she asked. "I wasn't even thinking when I came home without Steve. Don't worry, I can always ask the neighbors to drop you off."

My mom was at home, alone like she wanted to be. I was pretty sure she would hang up if I called her for a ride, and I didn't want one from a stranger. "Yeah," I said, "I'm sure she can." I faked a phone call, and waited while Mrs. Silverman dug through her purse and handed me a couple of twenties.

"Would you like me to wait with you on the porch?" she asked.

"Oh, no!" I said. "That's fine. She'll be here in a minute."

"Thank you so much," she said. "Sorry I surprised you earlier! Have a good night, sweetie!" As soon as she closed the door behind me I turned and watched through the frosted glass panel as she ran upstairs again. I didn't get it. Max was asleep. What was she going to do? Just sit next to him in the dark?

I waited a minute and then took off walking.

When I let myself in, my mom was on the couch, staring slightly above the TV, which was on as usual. "Well, look who's back," she said, smiling. She put her drink down on the coffee table and left the room, came back from the kitchen with another drink in her hand.

"You already have one here," I said, then regretted it. I didn't know what would make her turn on me anymore. But she didn't get mad this time.

"I know," she said. "It's for you. You can take care of a kid, you're old enough to drink. No fun drinking alone, anyway!" She handed me the glass.

I hadn't had anything to drink since Starr's. My mom didn't know about Starr and me drinking, and I liked that. This was vodka though. There was orange juice in there too, but not much, because I could see through the liquid, murky like seawater. I stood there, just holding it. She clinked her glass against mine, and a little bit spilled out. "Cheers," she said, and brought the glass to her mouth. I did the same.

I lost track of how many times she refilled our glasses. They were never empty, so it never felt like another whole drink, just a little bit more. The ice began to melt, stopped clinking against the sides of our glasses, diluting the orange juice but somehow making the vodka more potent. She turned into a different type of person. Nicer. But the only person who was doing something different was me. I thought maybe this was how I could get to her. Maybe if we were both drunk together, we could get along.

I had no idea what time it was. I reached into my pocket to show her the money Mrs. Silverman had given me. I wanted to show her that I could be useful. I could be independent, too. Instead, I pulled out a fistful of purple underwear. *Fuck*, I thought. I'd forgotten I'd taken Mrs. Silverman's lingerie—it was so flimsy that it didn't even take up enough room in the pocket of my shorts to remind me.

My mom raised her eyebrows. "Paid you in underwear, did she?" I smiled. She was different. I was in on the joke this time. I wasn't the joke anymore.

"Nope. I took 'em," I said, trying to sound the appropriate amount of proud. I still wasn't sure how she'd feel about it— they were her customers too. "She had so many!" I said. "She's not going to miss them."

My mom shook her head. "Well, let's see," she said. I wasn't sure what she was asking.

"Go on, put 'em on! Let's see." I stood up to go to the bathroom, and my vision faded to black for a moment, but she grabbed my arm before I could go any further. "I'm your *mother*," she said. "You can change in front of me."

I undressed sloppily, trying not to topple over, and fastened the bra on the tightest setting, adjusted the underwear so they covered more of my butt. I'd thought I looked sexy in the mirror in the closet at Mrs. Silverman's, but when I looked down at my body in the fluorescent light, all I could see were things that were wrong with it—my stomach stuck out slightly. My breasts were just too small to completely fill out the cups. Everything was see-through. My mom said nothing for a little while—thirty seconds, a minute, I don't know. Time was blurring, bleeding from one moment to the next in a way I'd never felt before. I folded my arms across my chest.

"Not bad!" she said. "I better be the only other person who

sees you like that for a long time though, if you know what I mean." I did, but I didn't say anything, just started putting my clothes back on over the purple lingerie, leaving my white cotton underwear on the carpet. I sat back down, because I thought I might throw up if I stood any longer. My mom moved closer, and put her arm around me. "This is nice," she said, taking another long sip of her drink. It had been years since she'd touched me like that. "Mmmhm," I whispered, and curled up on the couch, resting my head on her lap.

I woke up the next morning on the couch, with an ache in my neck and a pounding headache. My blanket was tucked around me. The clock on the VCR told me it was only 6:46 a.m., so I tiptoed to the bathroom. My stomach heaved. In the bathroom mirror, I studied my face. The grainy texture of the couch pillow had left marks, little red indents that dotted my cheek. I hadn't moved at all in my sleep. The circles under my eyes were dark and purple.

Then I felt it. I pulled my hair back with an elastic and gripped the side of the sink and the wall while I threw up, over and over again. I switched on the fan to clear out the smell, hoping the noise hadn't woken my mom, and gargled with mouthwash. I smiled, despite how awful I felt, and walked gingerly back to the couch. Unfolding the pullout bed, I fell asleep again, head heavy with my first real hangover, to the memory of my mom reaching her arm around me.

13

I figured out which house it was from all the cars parked out front, but nobody acknowledged me when I walked in. I wasn't really sure why I'd gone. Boredom, I guess. My mom was working late and I didn't feel like spending another night in that apartment, lying on the couch and watching the minutes pass on the VCR. I found the kitchen quickly, grabbed a beer from the fridge, and knocked the top of the bottle hard against the edge of the counter. The cap fell off easily into my hand and I took a swig from the bottle, getting mostly foam. "That was pretty cool," someone said. I looked behind me. A boy stood in the doorframe of the kitchen with a red cup in his hand. I shrugged my shoulders.

"I guess," I said. He stayed where he was, blocking my way out, but not like he wouldn't have moved if I had asked.

"I mean, most girls would have just asked a guy to open it for them," he said.

I remembered the time when I'd walked into the kitchen one night to get some water because the bathroom tap was broken and I was thirsty and feverish from a summer cold. My mom had been in there with Daryl, about to open another beer, leaning on the counter like she was about to fall over.

"Hey, Cal, why don't you learn to open these for your mom? Just hit it on the side of the counter like this. This is a cool trick," she said, and knocked the top of the bottle against the edge of the counter. The bottle cap clinked on the tile floor and she kicked it aside, near the trashcan. "Just try it," she said, and grabbed me another bottle from the fridge. "You can open one for Daryl." I was eight. My forehead was hot and the cold medicine hadn't kicked in yet. I wanted water, and I wanted to go to bed.

"It's gonna break, Mom," I said.

"No it won't," she said again. "Just try it." I knew she'd get angry if I said no. She was showing off. I took the unopened bottle from her hand, and bumped it on the corner of the counter. Nothing happened. "Harder," she said.

"Jeanie, don't you think—" Daryl said, and she shushed him.

"I'm gonna break it, Mom," I said again.

"Just try it, Cal," she said. Then she looked at me like I was an adult and said, "You're always so afraid to try anything." I slammed it into the counter and the bottle shattered. Shards of brown glass gathered around my bare feet and the stale smell of beer filled the kitchen. The brown liquid spread quickly on the tile. "Goddamn it!" she said, and walked out of the room.

"Don't move," Daryl said, and lifted me up. He carried me to the bathtub and set me down. "Wash your feet off and get to bed. I'll clean up. Hey, don't cry. Don't cry, Cal." I wasn't crying because I was hurt. I was crying because he was so nice. It was weird how that could make you cry, just someone being nice to you when you didn't even deserve it.

"My mom taught me," I said to the boy, snapping back to this kitchen, this party, this conversation.

He looked surprised. "Cool," he said. "I'm KJ."

"I'm Callie," I said. He looked young. I mean, he looked my age. His nose was big and peppered with blackheads. Oily. I couldn't stop staring at it, which I guess was good because otherwise I would have been staring into his eyes. He had long eyelashes. My mom got so mad when she saw boys with long eyelashes. She'd point them out to me, little boys tugging on their mothers' shorts at the grocery store, or the skateboarders who hung out on the wheelchair ramp outside our building. "It's not fair, Cal," she'd say. "I bet he can't even wear sunglasses, his eyelashes are so long."

"You have long eyelashes," I said to KJ, because I realized we'd been quiet for a few seconds. Then I bit my lip. I did it because I was nervous but then I realized it looked like I was flirting. I hadn't kissed a boy yet. I hadn't told anyone that. Only Jazz had known, and that was back in seventh grade, when it was still normal if you hadn't kissed a guy. Ninth grade was different.

He laughed. "So, uh, who do you know here?"

"Nobody," I said. "Andie's in my homeroom. She invited me. But I don't really know anyone else." I was surprised Andie had invited me. I didn't think she knew who I was until one morning on the way out of class she told me she liked my shorts. I was wearing denim cutoffs. "I couldn't pull off shorts that short," she said. "But your legs are so long it works. I can almost see your ass, but it works."

I was still learning how girls talked to each other, how sometimes you couldn't tell if something was supposed to be a compliment or an insult. I was figuring out my body. I knew my shorts were short but I didn't have boobs and I thought my legs were nice.

"Thanks," I said. "Your hair's really pretty. Mine won't get that long." I was lying. I didn't know where it came from. I'd never tried to grow my hair that long. Andie smiled, then sighed. "It's such a pain to brush though."

I don't know, after Jazz there was always this separation between me and any other girls I could have been friends with. It didn't make sense that you could feel like you existed in a secret world with one other person, that there was some force field around the two of you that wouldn't let anybody else in, and then one day it could pop and it was as if you'd never even spoken to each other, much less peeled the sunburned skin from each other's backs or examined the pale tan-line triangles of your bare chests side by side in the bathroom mirror. And I knew it was my fault, but I didn't know how to fix it or where she was now or what she'd seen that day and I never wanted to know but at the same time I wanted to know it all if it meant she could forget it.

KJ had moved out of the doorway and was leaning on the counter beside me. "I came with some of the soccer guys," he said. I scraped at the label on the beer bottle. "Andie and Jackson are kinda going together, and he's one of my friends on the team, so she told him to bring some people." I was pretty sure that meant they were having sex but there was no way I could ask that so I just nodded.

I didn't know how to talk to guys. I didn't know how to talk to anyone. I mostly watched TV and drank with my mom at our apartment whenever she was there, which wasn't much. She was always at the restaurant, working or drinking with her coworkers off the clock. And when I was alone, I was reading library books or rummaging through the fridge, which was always empty and I don't know why I bothered, or staring at myself in the mirror, appraising my body, wondering when my legs had gotten this long, when my hips had started to hold up my jean shorts.

"So, um, it might be quieter outside," KJ said. Music had

started blaring from the living room, a song with a loud bass that thumped in my chest to a beat I couldn't quite get the hang of. "It's a nice night out. You wanna go out there with me?"

Sometimes my mom would bring home a jug of cheap sangria from Rainbow Mart on her way home from work and we'd drive out to the beach and catch the last hour of sun out the dashboard window, drinking sangria out of Styrofoam cups from the restaurant. "I'd rather have you drinking with me than out partying," she'd say. "I remember high school boys. You're much better off drinking with me."

I followed KJ out the sliding glass door onto the patio. There were a couple of guys fiddling with the grill, which didn't seem to be working. A table littered with red cups vibrated from the boom box that sat atop it, its legs wobbling back and forth on the patchy grass. A group of girls sprawled on deck chairs, passing a handle of vodka between them, a two-liter bottle of Diet Coke at their feet.

KJ jerked his head to the left, motioning at the shed in the corner of the yard. He shrugged, embarrassed. "Just as loud out here, I guess. I just wanted to get out of that house. It'll be quieter behind the shed." He took my hand and led me there. "I think you're real cute," he said, and I thought about Johnny, something I hadn't done in a long time. *Both of y'all are real cute.*

And then KJ was kissing me, sloppy but gentle. We both tasted like beer. I wasn't sure what to feel so I froze. He pulled away and said, "I'm sorry. We don't have to do this. God, I feel like an asshole." Then he looked down and shook his head, like a dog after a bath. "C'mon, I'll take you back inside."

I didn't want KJ to be nice. I didn't want him to take me back inside. I wanted to kiss him more. Sometimes when somebody was nice to me it made me want to cry. Or sometimes it made me want to be mean to them, just to see how much they would let me.

I put a finger under KJ's chin and tipped it up again, forcefully. I kissed him and I knew what to do with my lips this time. He pulled away and took a deep breath. "I wasn't expecting that." I felt him through his jeans. I was someone else. I fumbled for his zipper. We were still behind the shed, rustling in the weeds while the party raged on around us. I stuck my hand down his boxers. "Wait," he said, but I pushed him against the shed with my other hand and pinned him to the wall. I wanted to see what he would let me do to him.

I didn't want to get drunk with my mom and it wasn't like she made me but sometimes she'd challenge me and I knew she didn't want to win. "C'mon," she'd say. "Finish your cup. Let me pour you another." Every time she drove us home I clutched the seatbelt to my chest so tightly that I had trouble unfurling my fingers after we made it across the bridge. Her hands were always light on the wheel, tapping along to the radio. She liked it loud, so loud I'd have to yell to get her to hear me. She'd get real close to the bumper of the car in front of us, then look over at me and smile, as if she knew it scared me. She did know.

And then I was on top of him, in the dirt, all of my weight pressing down on him. He could have flipped me over if he'd tried. I mean, he was tall and he played soccer. He was strong. But I think he was still surprised. I was a girl and I was tall but I was skinny, and not as tall as him, and I was holding him down in the patchy grass of someone else's backyard where anybody could have seen us if they'd walked around the shed. He looked like he liked the surprise of it. And I liked how it felt to be on top.

I pushed myself up so I was sitting on him. "We can go back inside, if you want," he said. I shook my head, grabbed his hand and put it inside my shirt.

"Take my shirt off," I said. I was wearing an old tank top and a bra I'd borrowed from my mom. It was black and lacy and I knew it looked good.

Sometimes it was, "Cal, I have to drive. You finish it." She knew I would, because if I didn't, she would. She took me to a meeting with her once, back when she'd tried to quit. I was too young to go to the one for family members by myself. Most of it was sad and boring but I couldn't help but remember some of the words from the packet they handed me on the way out, the terms they used. Were you an enabler? A hero? A mascot? A scapegoat? I was the only one she had. I was all of them. But I remembered this one sentence like it was burned into my brain. "The enabler often provides excuses for the alcoholic's behavior." Like it was my fault.

"Are you sure?" KJ asked. He looked confused. Like he was getting what he wanted but he didn't think it was happening. So I took off my top by myself. I let him watch me. I made him watch me.

"Your turn," I said, and lifted up the hem of KJ's shirt. The weeds must have been scratchy against his back but he didn't say anything, and he lifted his arms obediently for me. I pressed myself against him, and kissed him. Then I bit his lip, hard. He wasn't saying anything. I had never felt this kind of hardness beneath me before, but I knew what it meant, even though I'd never kissed a guy before tonight I knew what it meant, and I was grinding on top of him and he was saying "we can wait" and then I was undoing his belt and slipping my underwear to the side underneath my skirt and then he was saying something but it was like I was in a different world and I covered his mouth with one hand and slipped him inside of me with the other and he didn't want to like it but he did and I was moving harder, and the music was loud and nobody knew where we were, and beneath my hand he moaned and then it was over.

KJ looked at me kind of funny, in my bra and skirt on top of him. He said, "I didn't know you were like that." He paused. "It was my first time?" He said it like a question. He looked meaner now. "I just didn't want to lose it to a slut," he said, and sat up, shoving me roughly off of him. He wiped himself off on his shirt, then put it back on and walked away.

My tank top was on the ground. I picked it up, shook it off, put it back on. Liquid seeped through my underwear and dripped down my leg. It hadn't hurt and I hadn't bled. I leaned back against the shed. I knew he would tell his friends, leaving out one important detail. That was okay. I would know how to handle them. I would be the one in charge from now on.

14

My mom was still working at the Oasis and I was praying she didn't fuck it up because things were finally going well for me. I was sixteen and still weighed less than the minimum requirement for donating blood. I had the third-highest GPA in my high school class, and I pretended not to care about it but really I did. After KJ had told everyone what had happened at Andie's party, none of the guys at school wanted anything to do with me, or at least, didn't want to admit it. That was okay. Sometimes one of the soccer guys would hiss 'slut' at me in the hallway but I think they did that to any girl they knew wouldn't fuck them. I was surprised at all the ways it didn't make me feel.

One thing I hadn't expected was that I was now friends with Andie. In homeroom the Monday after her party, she'd sat down on the side of my desk and rolled her eyes. "So, KJ's an ass, huh?" she said, and I nodded. "Hey—you never sit with anyone at lunch." I hadn't thought anyone had noticed that I sat alone outside unless it was raining, reading and pretending to eat a bag of chips. "Come sit with me and Dawn today," she said. And that was it.

———————

It was better than being alone. I'd had enough of being alone.

I'd also discovered it was easier to make friends when you could drink with them. Friendship, according to the girls I'd gotten to know, seemed to be essentially just a way to share a secret with someone else, obtain absolution for whatever you'd done, and—in turn—receive a piece of gossip equally as dark and shameful as what you'd just divulged. It wasn't so much of a conversation as it was a mutual confession. So in that way, yes, I had friends. And there were other ways of not being alone.

My teachers were starting to talk about college now. I'd noticed that they always asked us what we wanted to be—never what we wanted to do—when we 'grew up,' as if some of us hadn't already grown up in ways more intimate and fucked-up than the rest of our adult lives would be. It seemed as if they believed that all we had to do was follow some formula and within ten years, we'd have jobs—not jobs, *careers*. The girls, especially, all seemed to be full of plans for the future that were, to me, impossibly grandiose and sad. Just because you could sew a decent apron in home ec didn't mean you were destined to live in New York City and become a famous fashion designer. I was embarrassed for them. I wasn't going to be like that. I forced any thoughts I had about the future to the back of my brain, where they shrank amidst the clutter of my immediate wants and desires, the needs of my day-to-day existence. That felt like a more honest way to live, somehow.

What if you'd already seen so many people living the lives they would have never dreamed for themselves that you didn't see any reason to believe it would be any different for you? No one wanted to still be a waitress when they were my mom's age. Someone had to do it. But nobody my age wanted to think that was how they'd end up. What if the way you were living was already as much as you could do?

I worked three nights a week at a pizza restaurant ten minutes away from our apartment. Every shift I would split a bottle of cheap cabernet—stolen, although we didn't like to think of it that way, from the boxes of overstock behind the restaurant bar—with a waitress in her early twenties who would take the bottle to the walk-in freezer and split it between two Styrofoam cups. I was the hostess, although the restaurant wasn't fancy enough to call it that; there, I was the phone girl.

We were at Andie's place, getting ready for the night. Andie had invited a couple of guys we'd met at the beach to spend the night at her place. Andie's mom was out of town. She was always out of town. There were three of us, and three of them.

"I get the hot one," Andie said, as if saying it would make it so. I was wearing a sundress. Andie and Dawn wore cutoffs. We scrutinized our own outfits, then each other's, in the wall mirror by the kitchen. "Is this too much?" I said. I wanted them to say no. I loved that dress. I'd saved up for it—I thought it made me look like I actually had tits. "You can borrow something," Andie said.

I changed into cutoffs, borrowed a Van Halen concert tee from Andie's older brother, soft and full of holes.

Getting ready with Andie and Dawn was different than getting ready with Starr. Starr had applied makeup like she was painting with acrylics, mixing different colors and liquids on the surface of her skin until it didn't look like she'd added anything, until all the colors had blended into each other. She was careful, precise, while her hair was feathered and soft.

Andie and Dawn did nothing to their hair—they both wore it parted in the center, long and sometimes greasy. With makeup, they were definitive, sloppily deliberate, jostling for mirror space. Andie lined her eyes, circling the inner and outer lids over and over again, until they were rimmed in thick, smudgy black liner that felt like paste and smeared slightly throughout the night. She thought her eyes looked beady without it.

Dawn wore mascara every day, obsessively, and combed out her eyelashes after applying it, then curled them, blow-drying the eyelash curler before using it, wincing slightly when the hot metal touched the paper-thin skin of her eyelids. Dawn looked perpetually wide awake, surprised, doe-like.

On her lips, she wore clear, shiny gloss that came in a tube she kept in her pocket, which she took out frequently and reapplied incessantly, sometimes to the point where she'd open her mouth to speak and strings of lip gloss would stretch from the top to bottom lip in both corners of her mouth. She was obsessed with looking natural, in the way that a lot of girls with bad skin seem to be. She had the kind of pimples that stayed underneath the surface, bumps that didn't turn red or come to a head, but just made the surface of her skin uneven. She tried valiantly to combat it, scrubbing her face raw with Noxzema every night and applying layers of foundation every morning, on top of which she dusted powder in an attempt to smooth everything out. Despite this, Dawn was beautiful, but she hated herself and I'd recently learned that this was something men could sense.

I'd heard my boss talking to one of the drivers about the new girl he was dating a couple months after I'd started working there. "Gotta find a girl with bad skin. I mean, hot, but, *bad skin*, man, I'm telling you," he said, hitching up his pants with the hand that wasn't holding the pizza paddle. "Girls like that don't think they're pretty. They'll do anything." He laughed to himself, obviously remembering something he'd convinced this girl to do, the lack of confidence that he'd exploited.

I thought to myself how dangerous it could be to set your value at what you thought you might deserve.

15

They liked me at the restaurant because I was young and pretty but I wasn't dumb, and I worked hard. I did the shit jobs and ran errands for everyone and I covered for myself as well, even when I was drunk out of my mind. Everyone there was drunk or high out of their minds, or both.

But when the boss did stop by, everybody was on their best behavior. Janet and Amara would hastily slip on the baggy uniform shirts over their tank tops and pull back their hair. We'd pop a breath mint, pour out our Styrofoam cups, cursing if we'd just filled them, or we'd hide them in the walk-in behind a giant jar of tomato sauce. We stood up straight instead of slouching, greeted everyone who walked in. The drivers actually pulled into the lot instead of doing a half-ass parking job on the dirt. We were all intimidated by the boss.

The boss was a hefty, bearded man who always showed up drunk and wearing safari gear—khakis with lots of pockets, canvas hat, that type of shit. He looked like the picture of Hemingway on the back of my copy of *The Sun Also Rises*, which we were reading in English class now. His wife had been a frail, pinched woman who died shortly after I began working there.

When he hired me, he'd tucked a stray lock of my hair behind my ear and said, "You know, you remind me of my wife when we first met." I hadn't said anything but I'd given him what I hoped was a sympathetic look, my eyes wide and sad, my lips curled into an almost smile.

Occasionally, he'd call me into the office and give me generous raises, saying, "You're really getting the hang of things around here." It was a while before I realized nobody else's pay had gone up two dollars an hour every month during what would turn out to be a particularly slow summer. After I realized this, I did whatever I could to ensure that it kept happening. I kept it a secret but I wasn't ashamed.

Sometimes when I got really drunk, I thought about how things had worked out for my mom, nearing forty and working nights at a waterfront restaurant where jackass tourists sat underneath brightly colored umbrellas while their children splashed unattended in a pool that hadn't been cleaned once since she'd begun working there. A restaurant where leathery old men brushed her ass with their hands as she walked past the bar as a way of requesting a refill. Where the most popular drink was a twenty-ounce margarita with five drops of blue food coloring added at the end. I knew I was working in food service too. But I was smarter than she was. I was an asshole about it, but I was smart.

When I walked into the guidance counselor's office for my college consultation, she'd raised her eyebrows. I was wearing cut-offs so old and frayed that the pockets poked out from below the hem. My shirt was from the thrift store across from our apartment complex, black and lacy and sheer. Underneath, I was wearing a red bra. My hair was teased, three days unwashed, and pulled into a big side braid that I'd slept on the night before.

I wouldn't get in trouble if I wore clothes like that. I knew my name was on the list of students from 'unstable home environments' who had 'potential.' If I'd ever bothered to eat school lunch other than once a month when I caved and bought a slice of pizza then threw it up in the bathroom afterward, Andie holding my hair back, it would have only cost me forty cents instead of two dollars. I would have had to do something really bad to actually get in trouble.

"So, Calliope, have you given any thought to college?" she asked me, pointedly avoiding looking anywhere below my eyes. "With these grades and test scores, you've got quite a future. If you want it."

I put my feet up on her desk, revealing chipped red nail polish and cork wedges. I was starting to treat every encounter like a potential seduction, even when I didn't mean to. I raised my eyebrows at her, at once daring her to tell me to take my feet down and to let her know how ludicrous of a suggestion that was. In fact, I used that exact word. "Considering the amount of money college costs, that seems like a somewhat ludicrous suggestion," I said, crossing one leg over the other.

"Well, it's really not," she said. "For a girl as smart as you, there are many scholarships available. I'm available to help you apply for as many as you want." She handed me a piece of paper with a list of names and amounts and requirements.

"This seems like a lot of work," I said, and shoved it into my purse. She sighed.

"You're incredibly bright, Callie," she said. "This is an opportunity. We'll find a way to make things work for you." She pressed her hands down on the stacks of paper on her desk and began to stand up. "I can tell I'm not going to make any progress today, but let me leave you with this. Not everyone is trying to screw you over. And you're not going to get a better chance to use your intelligence to get you where you want to be than this. So come back when you want to talk some more." I swung my legs down.

"Thanks," I said, "but I don't need your fucking pity." I didn't even turn to see the expression on her face when I walked out.

I was driving Andie's car because I could hold my alcohol the best out of the three of us, even though I was the skinniest. That was another thing I pretended not to care about but really did. I wasn't a lightweight.

The sun warmed my left arm through the driver's side window. I wanted to be at Andie's already and I wanted to drive along the water with the setting sun and my two friends forever. We were getting close. There was beer in the fridge and liquor in the cabinet. We had couches and empty rooms. It was a Saturday night.

It didn't feel like a problem at the time, and I don't think I ever called it what it was. I never got skinny enough to where I looked like I was starving, never stopped getting my period. Anorexia was for the rich girls anyway, the ones who sat hunched over miserably at the corner table in the cafeteria, the bony bumps down their spine visible underneath their tank tops. The ones who packed carrot sticks and celery stalks for lunch, dipping them listlessly into impossibly small containers of ranch dressing. That wasn't the way I operated. I didn't eat much, but I ate what I wanted when I wanted, so sometimes throwing up just seemed like the best idea. It was direct, easier, sloppy—no planning involved. I could fix a mistake just like that, instead of trying every goddamn hour of the day not to make any mistakes at all.

If I threw up, I could have it both ways, eat a whole small pizza at work, happy and drunk, without even noticing. Then I could take a smoke break, lock myself in the family bathroom, and stick my finger down my throat, keeping it there until my gut roiled and every half-digested slice of Italiansausageextracheesewelldone came back up in chunks, sometimes so freshly consumed that it even tasted good on the way back up, in a way that only vaguely disgusted me. Afterward, my throat was a little sore, but it didn't matter, because I was empty again, ready for more—ready for anything.

Whenever my manager, Corey, talked about women in front of me, he'd preface his remarks with an apology. "No offense, Callie. So, Mike, listen—I fucked this chick in the bathroom at 600 North last night, and we almost broke the sink," he'd say, shoving the paddle into the oven to remove a pizza, or switch it to another shelf. Beads of sweat from the heat formed along his hairline. His forearms were red, flushed from the heat of the oven. "I'm not offended," I'd tell him, and I wasn't. I thought I was better than the girls Corey talked about, which was arrogant and ultimately untrue. Corey was the kind of man who took the newspaper with him to the bathroom at the restaurant and told everyone, "Hold my calls—I'll be a while." I thought I was better than these men because I knew when to be ashamed of myself. Even that turned out to be untrue.

There were so many pathetic men working at that restaurant that sleeping with some of them almost felt like doing them a favor. And if they slipped their tips in the back pocket of my jeans at the end of their shift, I didn't complain. Mitch was a driver in his mid-forties. He wore gym shorts that he'd won in a contest at a strip club, the name of the club embroidered on the bottom corner of the left leg. I didn't ask what he'd done to win them but after I fucked him in his car in the apartment parking lot next to the restaurant he started wearing them a lot more often. He didn't even have to unbutton anything, just slip them down. Mitch was also a substitute teacher at my school. He never subbed any of my classes, but once I saw him in the hall. He was about to say hi, but I was with Andie and Dawn and made it clear that I would pretend I had never seen him in my life. Out of a sense of competition—not dignity—we only talked about the hot ones, the ones we had to work for, somewhat. Mitch was not one of those men.

Andie still had parties at her mom's house all the time. But they were smaller now, and most of the guys who came, if they'd gone to our high school, had graduated long ago. The boys we went to high school with had no potential but they still had a chance to become something, especially if they were rich—they'd take over their fathers' companies, somehow graduate with a two-year degree and make money through pyramid schemes that only idiots fell for.

The men we invited over had demonstrated years ago that they had no potential, and their chances were up. These men were infinitely more interesting to us. It was so much easier to manipulate a thirty-five-year-old man who still lived with his brother over a bar into giving you what you wanted than it was to get an eighteen-year-old boy, one who thought he was going places, to do *anything* for you.

My mom was dating the manager of the Oasis now. She was barely ever home, and if she was, she was so wasted she barely even knew who I was. "Frank, this is, this is my daughter and I love her and—" She couldn't even remember my name. But she left me alone. And she didn't make me drink with her anymore. And for that, I could not thank Frank enough, no matter how many lingering glances he gave me before they disappeared into her room.

Most of the time it didn't bother me. Most of the time I was drunk, happy, drifting, flirting with customers over the phone or deep into a book or wiping my mouth after swallowing, concealing the half-smile that came with knowing I'd just given some loser the best blow job of his life. But sometimes when I was sober and alone at the apartment I cycled through all of the grimy bathrooms, the filthy bedrooms, the messy backseats of shitty old cars, and everything I'd done inside them.

It was like how dust gathered in the corners of a room, and you didn't notice it or think about it until one day you decided to move the furniture or something and then it was all there, clumped and dirty, and no matter how many times you tried to sweep it all up there was always a little bit that wouldn't go away and you had to sweep it back under the sofa where it was before but now you knew it was there, and the floor always felt gritty under your feet from then on.

16

I don't know if she would apologize for it if she knew where I was, or how to get in touch with me. I mean, a real apology, one that makes it clear that she understands what she did and what it did to me. But she won't get that chance. I won't give it to her.

Last I heard from Carmen, who worked with my mom at the Oasis, my mom was in AA—again—but it was sticking this time, apparently. Frank wasn't there anymore, but my mom still was, diligently refusing any pre-, during-, and post-work drink offers, which is hard to do at a restaurant, especially one like the Oasis. I trusted Carmen to tell me the truth. I also trusted her not to tell my mom where I was.

I'd pulled a disappearing trick, just like my mom had done so many times before. That was one trait I hadn't expected to inherit.

I could say it was alcohol that made her do it, and I might be right. But the worst part of it is I think she would have had it in her to do it stone-cold sober. And I wonder if that's the kind of person I'm going to turn out to be. Marcus says it's not. He says if you grow up with shitty parents you become the kind of person you wish your parents had been. I hope he's right. I mean, I think that's bullshit about a lot of people, but I hope he's right about me.

I wasn't even supposed to be home that night. Andie and Dawn and I had plans to get shitfaced with a few guys who worked at our favorite bars downtown. They were fun, but mostly we were hoping that if they got to know us a little bit, we wouldn't have to show IDs anymore when they were working. But Andie's mom only got as far as the airport before she turned around and came right back, crying, and without a job—her boss's wife had found out about their affair, which was news both to her boss's wife and to Andie. "Don't come over," Andie said over the phone to me and Dawn. "It'll just make things worse. Just— call those guys, tell them we'll hang out another time." So I was home on a Friday night for the first time in a while.

I didn't know what to do with myself when I was alone, really. I hated being alone. All I could think about were bad things. If I was alone I did everything in my power to distract myself. Half the time that involved whatever alcohol my mom had laying around but just as often it involved a book. The library wasn't far from our apartment, and I'd just discovered John Cheever and Raymond Carver and it felt good to read about someone else's fucked up life rather than think about my own. So that's what I was doing, sober, when my mom and Frank stumbled into the living room, wild-eyed and talking loud and grasping onto each other like they were running a three-legged race. I sat up, tossed my book to the side, gave them a nod.

"Oh, hon, I thought you were going to be out tonight!" my mom said. "We were just gonna have some drinks here, a little party for two. We won't keep you up though. We can go in the bedroom." My bed was still the pull-out couch in the living room. The apartment was so small I knew I'd hear them wher-ever they were.

"No, it's okay," I said, gathering my book and my bowl of mac and cheese. "I'll just sleep in your room tonight. You guys can have the rest of the apartment." *Just a couple more months*, I reminded myself, but then I thought, *a couple more months until what?* I'd effectively alienated my guidance counselor, I hadn't applied to any colleges, and I wasn't even sure I could switch to full-time at the restaurant after I graduated. I had money saved, but nothing crazy. Graduation was in just a couple months. And then what?

"You're the best, Cal," she slurred, dragging Frank down onto the couch. Frank's balding head shone under the lamp on the side table. I wasn't sure why she was dating him, but then again, I wasn't sure why she'd dated any of the men she brought home. Except for Daryl, but that was years ago. I tried not to think about Frank fucking my mom but I couldn't help it. Was she dating him so he would go easy on her at work? My mom was still attractive, despite what a life like hers will do to you. But that was really her only option, to keep being pretty. Pretty used to be a way out but she was past that. Now her kind of pretty was just a way to keep going.

Frank sat up. "It's okay, Cal. Why don't you stay out here for a little while? It's absolutely criminal how little I know about you." He smiled wide, like his face would crack in half if he held it too long. I stood there. I couldn't read my mom's expression, didn't know if she wanted me to get out or stay, like Frank had asked. But I didn't know how I was going to sleep if they were out there anyway. "Sure," I said.

For a long time I didn't know how to say what had happened. After a certain point I'd stopped saying no, but worse than that, I'd tried. There was some sick part of me that had wanted him to not be able to forget me. The worst part was my mom watching, and not saying anything. No, it was that she did say something, in the beginning, that it was *well, we're so drunk we won't even remember,* that it was *why not?,* that it was *well, this'll be a story.* The worst part was that.

It was like those dares she used to give me—when she'd make me finish the rest of the sangria before we drove home, when she'd speed up just to scare me. Except this wasn't a dare or a challenge, no matter what they said. I couldn't get out of this.

The weirdest thing was what I was thinking about while it was happening—this one day in middle school science class, during a unit on geology. "Those pebbles you find on the beach used to be much larger pieces of rock," Mr. Gonzalez had said. "It can take thousands of years, but eventually, wind and water and sun will smooth a rock into a stone." Patience, I was thinking, as my mom watched what was happening and didn't say a word, all you need is patience. The rough edges will go away if you wait long enough.

I truly didn't know what I would have done if Marcus hadn't been there, if he and Daryl had moved, if a stranger had answered the door when I knocked. But it was Marcus, just as my twelve-year-old self had remembered him—tall and strong, with bulging muscles, and a smile that made you feel like you were the only person that mattered to him. "Calliope!" he said, and pressed me to his chest, and let me cry, just like that, in the doorway, until I was ready to speak.

"I can't believe it," he said when I was done. "I mean, I can, but—goddamn. She just got worse, didn't she?" I nodded. We were sitting at the table, sharing some leftover Chinese food. "Look, about that one time," I said, "right before we left—"

"Cal." He stopped me. "You were *twelve*. You didn't know what you were doing. Honestly, I was dealing with some issues of my own at the time.

"I'm good now, though," he continued. "I'm still manager, but just part-time now. I'm actually back in school—getting a degree in business, if you can believe it. I might open my own place one day, even." He raised his eyebrows and grinned.

"Where's Daryl?" I asked. I felt uncomfortable. It wasn't like I was scared to see Daryl, but I didn't exactly want him to come home to some part of his past that had left him behind, crying at his kitchen table.

"Daryl got his own place. I got the trailer." He sensed my worry but got the reason wrong. "He wouldn't be angry that you're here, Cal. You know that, right?" I nodded. "So, you took the bus from Daytona, huh?" he said. "Bet you met a lot of crazies."

I had taken the bus, but I'd kept to myself, Walkman on my lap and headphones on, even after the batteries had died. I'd worn my baggiest jeans and oldest t-shirt, and sneakers I only used for work. I'd hitched a ride from the bus depot to Marcus and Daryl's old address, surprised at how easily it sprang to my tongue.

Marcus reached his hands across the table, like he was going to put them on mine, but just placed them down gently in front of me. "I'm so glad you came," he said. "You can crash on my couch as long as you want. You're safe here." I didn't know what to say.

Frank poured us shots of vodka, and brought the bottle back to the coffee table. My mom turned on the stereo, and started dancing her way back to the couch, which wasn't really big enough for the three of us. She was still wearing her serving apron. "This is fun, right?" she said, like she was trying to convince herself. "I never get to drink with you, Cal!" If she'd come home like this alone, I would have made her some toast like usual, sat with her while she drank a glass of water, put her to bed.

"Bottoms up!" Frank said, and slapped my mom's ass before she sat down. We tipped our shot glasses in unison and swallowed. The sweet burn as it shot down my throat relaxed me, almost instantly.

I was hoping I was wrong about what Frank wanted to know but after a few questions about school he moved straight to the subject of men. "I know you and your mother are very close," he said, clapping a hand on one of each of our thighs. "No secrets here, right?" I couldn't begin to answer what he assumed was a rhetorical question. "So—how are the boys at Seabreeze? Got a *beau*?" He grinned. "Going steady?"

I stared at him. "No," I said, in the calmest voice I could muster. "No beau, Frank. I like being alone."

"Oh, but you certainly seem to spend enough time with men who *don't* go to your high school!" my mom said, with a false cheerfulness. I felt sick.

"What do you mean by 'spend time,' exactly?" I said, and poured myself another shot.

"Whoa, there!" Frank said. "Save some for the rest of us!" He poured out two more for my mother and him.

"You know what I'm talking about. I'm not around much, but I'm not blind. Doesn't help that about three different strangers have asked me if I have a sister named Cal—somewhat shocking to hear that from a man at a bar you shouldn't even be legally allowed into."

I didn't know what to say. I didn't feel like I needed to defend myself.

"Ladies… let's calm down," Frank said. "I was just curious. Now I know. So she likes the older men, Jeanie—no harm in that! I've got a few years on you myself," he said, and winked. "Like mother, like daughter."

"She's seventeen, Frank," my mom said, and started to drink from the bottle. I raised my eyebrows. It was going to be a long night.

He held out his hand for the bottle, and after a long drink, passed it to me. I hesitated for a moment. But if I was going to keep hanging out with them, I wanted to keep my buzz going. So I drank. My mac and cheese was congealing, uneaten, on the side table.

After Marcus went to bed, I lay awake on the couch, using a couple of beach towels as a makeshift blanket. I felt guilty about how nice he was being to me, that same feeling I always had when people were nice to me, how it either made me want to cry, or it made me want to be mean. Except now it also made me want to make it up to him. I couldn't stay there forever. And I wanted to get out of this fucked-up place, this whole fucked-up state. I counted my cash. Enough for now. But not for long.

Things get blurry when your mother and her boyfriend are basically pouring vodka down your throat, into your empty stomach. I'm not sure when Frank's pants came unzipped, not sure when the conversation tipped so that Frank's suggestion didn't seem disgusting or ridiculous but like something natural, something that wouldn't even be a big deal. I'm not sure how many times

I said no before I just shut up. I remember brief moments, flashes—Frank calling me a little slut, my mom running to the bathroom to vomit before he'd even pulled his underwear up again, how he tried halfheartedly to pin me down on the couch afterward, brushing the hair from my face before I shoved him off and went to check on my mom. My mom screamed out, "Fuck you, Frank!" from where she sat, curled into the corner between the bathtub and the wall. He left while we were still in the bathroom.

When Marcus came home from work a couple nights after I'd arrived, I was wearing my shortest skirt, platform sandals, and my mom's pink halter top, one of the few things I'd taken when I left. I'd made spaghetti but I had no intention of eating it; however, I'd left the sauce simmering on the stove because I thought the scent made the trailer seem comfortable, more like a home. I was drinking rum with a splash of Coke, and I'd even cut up a lime to put on the rim of the glass, like bartenders did when it wasn't too busy. There was another drink waiting for Marcus on the counter.

I heard his car rattling up next to the trailer, and I stood on my tiptoes to see my reflection in the microwave. I'd managed to find the lipstick my mother used to wear with that top, Revlon Softshell Pink, and I'd used the crappy travel blow-dryer under the sink (I wasn't an idiot; of course there had been other women here) to try out a floaty hairstyle with a wavy side part that I'd seen on a model on the cover of some magazine. I remembered the last time I'd seen Marcus, before we'd left Tampa again, and how proud I'd been to have those silky black straps slipping out from under my tank top and onto my shoulders, when I hadn't even needed a bra. This time I wasn't wearing one.

Marcus seemed confused when he walked in, but after he sat down with a big bowl of spaghetti and his drink he looked genuinely happy. "You've outdone yourself, lady," he said. As soon as his drink was empty, I refilled it, and mine too, taking more and more effort to walk steadily on my platforms each time. Back on the couch, I stretched out my legs in front of me, marveling at how far they could reach. I was a bit drunk. I was going to say thank you to Marcus, so I wouldn't feel guilty anymore.

When Marcus said he was heading for bed, I widened my eyes and looked up at him. "So soon?" I asked, and ran a finger underneath the strap of the halter top, a movement he could interpret however he liked.

"Wish I could keep you company, Cal, but it's almost midnight, and I've got class early tomorrow. Hey, if you leave the dishes to soak, though, I'll do them in the morning." He stood there for just a beat longer than usual, and I took that as my cue. Finally I'd feel as if I were good for something. I stood up—in my platforms, I was almost as tall as him—wrapped my arms around him, and kissed him, hard. And within a second, he pushed me away, just like he'd done so many years ago.

"What the hell are you doing, Cal?" he asked, genuinely confused.

"I just thought—" I bit my lip, feeling what was left of my lipstick slide off onto my teeth. This wasn't how it was supposed to go. No man had said no to me in a very long time. "I didn't know why else you would let me stay here if you didn't want—" I was too shy now to even say it. "If you didn't think—" I said quietly. "—I mean, I'm not twelve anymore. And I wanted to thank…" I lost my train of thought. "I don't even know," I said, tearing up.

"Oh god," Marcus said. "Is that why you thought I was letting you stay? Because I thought I'd *get* something from you? You have no idea how awful that makes me feel."

Feeling pathetic, but just bold and numb enough from the rum to think it was still a worthwhile pursuit, I tried one more time, kissing his neck. "Don't you *want* me?" I asked. He backed away again and sank into the couch, looking unbearably sad, just as he had when I'd last tried to get close to him. But there were more layers to his sadness this time. And more to mine.

"If you were anyone else? Of course I'd want you," Marcus said. "Sit down." I obeyed, kicking off my platforms and tucking my feet underneath me. "Look at me," he said, and I did.

"Cal, there are no strings attached here. You're here because you need to be, and because I like having you around. But not like that. Jesus, I've known you for what, ten years? Since you were a little kid. I saw how it was with your mom. I just want you to feel like you have someone on your side. Like me." Then he smiled. "So don't try that shit again."

I'd never imagined he would say no to me. But somehow it made sense. And it felt right that he had never wanted anything from me, that I would have been drawn to him precisely for that reason. I felt, more than ever, that this had been the right place to run to. I realized he was waiting for a reaction from me. "I'm so sorry," I said. "I'm an idiot. But—will you just hold me? Just for a minute?" He nodded, and I leaned back into him, closing my eyes, until I felt my shoulder being shaken. I'd fallen asleep.

"All right, I'm *really* going to bed this time," Marcus said. He filled up a big glass of water and left it by the couch. "You'll want that when you wake up. Goodnight, Calliope," he said, then disappeared into the bedroom.

In the morning, Marcus made coffee and eggs for me before he headed off to school, and then I was alone again, that awful heaving loneliness that was worse than it had ever been before.

When she was done throwing up, she curled up on the bathroom rug, now flecked with her vomit. I went to get her some water, and when I came back she was sitting on the toilet, with the lid closed. She wouldn't even look at me. "Leave it on the sink and get out," she said. I put the glass down and stood there.

"Get. Out. Did you not hear me? I don't want to *see* you when I leave this bathroom. You're a whore." She spat out those last words. "Don't think I don't know what you're up to when you're not here. At least I have a boyfriend. You fuck anybody who you think gives a shit about you. But guess what? They don't. They just want to fuck you. Don't think you're special because you're young and you're pretty. I hope you get pregnant, I really do. I hope you end up with a daughter just like you, so you know what it's like. You'll be old and fat and ugly and alone and then you'll know what it feels like, then maybe you'll have a fucking ounce of sympathy for me, for what you think I've 'done' to you." She'd exhausted herself. She dropped to the floor and curled up on the rug again. I wanted to sit next to her and stroke her hair, despite myself. But instead I listened. And I left.

Marcus never mentioned that night again. I'd tried to apologize when he got home from work the next evening, but he stopped me. "There's nothing to apologize for," he said, and there was a kindness in his voice that let me know he really meant it.

Every morning on his way out, while I was still asleep on the couch, he'd leave a cup of coffee in the pot for me. During the day I'd wander my old neighborhoods until I was sweating through my clothes, then I'd duck into the Publix on Gandy and shiver as the sweat dried instantly on my skin. With his money, I'd buy groceries for the both of us, and have something ready for dinner whenever he got home. I usually made something healthy, but sometimes I'd buy a box of Hamburger Helper, and stick a wet finger in the seasoning packet to take a lick before I poured it into the pan. No matter what I made, Marcus ate everything on his plate.

Most nights, we'd settle in on the couch, Marcus and me

curled up on opposite sides, and pick something stupid to watch on TV. On the weekends, he let me drive his car to the library, and I'd pick out enough books to last me for the week. Then, after he'd gone to bed, I'd stay up late, reading by the anemic glow of the goldfish tank and the light above the oven. But I still felt like I was waiting for something—this wasn't a life I could live forever. I needed the possibility of a future or else I felt like I'd die on that couch. I woke up shaking at three in the morning from a nightmare where I looked like my mother but thirty years in the future—wrinkly, shrunken and bony, rattling and gasping for air on that couch as Marcus, youthful and handsome as ever, held my hands as I died. I needed to go somewhere.

The next morning, I took my notebook out of my backpack to plan out the rest of my life but then that seemed a little bit ambitious and I just started doodling all over the page instead. I ended up drawing hundreds of tiny stars, a jumble of constellations, the kind with five points that you learn how to draw as a little kid. I stared at the page for a minute, then picked up Marcus's phone and called information.

Amidst my doodled stars, I wrote down the number the woman on the other end of the phone had given me. I'd gotten lucky finding Marcus, but Eugene was a lot farther than Tampa. I knew where I wanted to be. I dialed the number and closed my eyes, praying for a ring.

17

Marcus understood that my leaving had nothing to do with him. I told him about Starr, but I didn't tell him what she meant to me, in part because I didn't know how to put it into words, and in part because I didn't really know.

And I'm sure it wasn't easy for him either, though I do believe he would have let me stay with him in that crowded trailer for as long as I needed. That was just the kind of person he was. Which made it even more bittersweet to leave.

We were slouched on the couch a couple nights before I was set to get on a plane and fly across the country for... for what? I didn't even know. For hope? I was sleepy, and my head was resting on Marcus's shoulder, in a way that I'd come to understand—and appreciate—would always be interpreted by him as completely platonic. The shows we'd been watching were long over, and an infomercial blared out at us from the television we'd been too lazy to turn off. The remains of dinner were on the coffee table, crumpled paper towels and the dregs of our rum and Cokes, ice long melted, the light brown liquid pooled in the bottom of the glasses. I was completely comfortable—just the right amount of drunk to hover on the side of sentimental rather than maudlin. He shook my thigh gently. "Cal, don't fall asleep just yet." I rolled my head in a lazy circle, then stood up and began to carry the dishes over to the sink. "I'm awake—what's up?"

"I just thought, your last day here is Thursday. We should... *do* something, you know? Go out to dinner. Somewhere nice. Or—what do you want to do before you leave? Where do you want to say goodbye to?" Though he didn't mean to, Marcus had made me incredibly sad. There was nothing I wanted more than to leave this place but remembering that I would likely not return for years, if ever, wasn't something I could think about for too long without doubting the plans I'd made.

"No dinner," I said. "I mean, no fancy dinner. That's not what I want for my last night."

"Fair enough," he said, tapping his fingers on his thighs like he was thinking hard about a better alternative. "Maybe the beach, then? One last sunburn? Watch the sunset? Sit in the dark and listen to the ocean?" After every option I'd shook my head. Nothing felt right and everything was painful. "Just sit on this damn couch?" he said finally, pretending to be fed up. "I got nothin'. You're gonna have to help me out."

My arms were submerged halfway in the soapy sink water, rinsing the last of the dishes. I looked down at my arms, freckled from years in the sun, and I had an idea.

"Let's get tattoos," I said. "Matching tattoos. That's what I want."

Marcus gave me a long look from the couch. "You must be drunker than I thought," he said. "You're joking, right?"

"No," I said, realizing only in that moment that I was completely serious. "I think it's a brilliant idea, actually." I smiled at him and raised an eyebrow. "Why, you scared?"

"I'm not scared," he said. "I have tattoos already. God knows anything you came up with would be better than some of this shit." He was right. There were some questionable decisions inked into his arms and legs that, on him, were endearing, but on anyone else I would have found off-putting. "But you've never gotten one. But..." he trailed off. "Yeah. I'll do it, if you're sure it's what you want."

The next evening, Marcus drove us to his friend Rafi's apartment. Rafi ran a tattoo studio out of his apartment but it was perfectly safe and professional, Marcus assured me. Rafi had done every other one of Marcus's tattoos.

Rafi opened the door with a smile, which I was grateful for, because the rest of his body was covered in tattoos, from the neck down, and I might have been intimidated otherwise. While Marcus and Rafi caught up, I paced between Rafi's kitchen and his living room, letting Rafi's pit bull sniff my legs then nuzzle up against me like he'd determined I wasn't a threat. I knelt down to rub his head, and he started to wag his tail vigorously, dog tags and choke chain clanking against each other. "Cal!" Marcus called from the other room. "Rafi's ready. Come on in here."

Rafi had turned his spare room into what looked like a fully functional tattoo parlor. It was dark in there—no windows, but there were fluorescent lights trained on the La-Z-Boy in the center of the room, and the tool kit beside it.

"So what are we getting?" Marcus said. *I have total trust in you*, he'd said earlier. *You pick; I'll get it.* I pulled out the drawings I'd traced from a book in the library earlier that day. "Constellations," I said. "Like you used to show me." Marcus looked at me like he wanted to say something, then registered Rafi's presence, as if he'd briefly forgotten we weren't the only two people in the room.

Rafi nodded. "Sweet. Won't be hard. Lemme take a look, draw it out in pen first so you can see if you like it. Who's going first?"

"I am," I said, and sat down. I held out my arm. "Let me show you the freckles I want you to use." I pointed to the freckles, and Rafi dotted them with a fine-tip marker. "I think that should work," I said. "I have a lot of freckles if you need to use different ones." Rafi looked back and forth from the drawing to my arm, nodded, and began to outline the constellation I'd chosen. Ursa Major. The giant bear. Ursa Major had been a woman and they'd hunted her straight into the sky, where Jupiter had transformed her into a bear. A million miles away and impervious.

Rafi popped a clean razor from a plastic container and shaved the hair from that patch of my arm, swabbing it with an alcohol wipe. All three of us were silent. He poured ink into little cups and set them on the table next to my chair, slid on a pair of blue latex gloves, and rubbed Vaseline into the skin on my arm. When he pulled out the needles to insert into the machine, I briefly, reflexively turned away, and Marcus put a hand on my shoulder to reassure me.

"This is a quick one. No color, just a couple of lines," Rafi said, gently grabbing my wrist to extend my arm toward him. "Won't be too bad. Really."

"I'm sure I've felt worse," I said. And that felt true, and comforting to me.

The underside of my arm was visible to me now that it was extended, and it reminded me of the belly of a fish, something you didn't always see—an unexpected view of a place that always felt vulnerable. My skin was soft and thin there.

When the needle grazed my skin, I breathed in sharply, but when Rafi paused midway to wipe away the blood, I realized that I hadn't even been paying attention to the pain at all. "All done," he said, pulling out a bandage to wrap around my arm. "Man, you didn't even flinch."

"She's tough," Marcus said. Rafi was cleaning already,

indifferent, distracted. "So which one did you pick for me?" Marcus asked. I handed him the paper.

"The Big Dipper," I said. "All seven stars. For showing me all of them." I studied his face, watching for his reaction.

"I'm gonna miss you," he said, sitting down in the La-Z-Boy. "That's for fucking sure."

18

I barely had anything with me, just my duffle bag, which was so empty it hung slack from my shoulder. I looked like I was spending the night away, not moving across the country. Again, it was strange what I'd thought to bring with me when I left— the inventory of items that were all I now had. A few pairs of jeans, low-slung and loose, stolen from some of the slimmer-hipped men's apartments and houses where I'd slept over the years. That old shirt of Daryl's, now so soft from washing that I felt it would disintegrate if I rubbed it between my fingers. That navy silk robe from Starr, which now fit me the way it was supposed to, clinging to my hips, hemline hitting just above my knee, nipples visible underneath the paper-thin fabric in certain lighting. The only outwardly feminine, sexy clothing I'd taken was my mother's. I don't know why. I knew that sometimes it came in handy to wear something tight, or maybe it was to spite her—or maybe it was more than that. Maybe I'd taken those particular items because they reminded me of a time when I'd been in charge; when we'd been a team, or it had at least felt that way. That pink halter top from the night we'd driven home from Daryl's together, when she'd crawled into my bed early the next morning to hold me. That old V-neck, stretchy and low-cut and faded now at the armpits, that she'd worn for days straight on that drive to Eugene. And, inexplicably, one of her Oasis polo shirts—ugly and cheap, with a scratchy embroidered logo on the left breast pocket.

I didn't have many books, any at all, really. But the day before I'd left, Marcus had given me three brand new paperbacks. "I know you're packing light," he said, "but here's something to start your collection with when you get there." He'd also given me a leather jacket that he said he'd found at the thrift store, but I'd found the tag from Burdines beside the trashcan. It was just another debt I would have to accept I couldn't repay—that I wasn't expected to repay. That was more important. I felt like I might need a lifetime to learn the true difference between a debt and a favor, and the difference between the kinds of people who could turn the same action into one or the other.

So it was in my new leather jacket, Daryl's old shirt, and someone else's jeans that I arrived at the airport. It was an early morning flight, but Marcus had still left for work before I'd woken up. We'd just said goodnight as usual the night before, both aware of the fact that we were pretending we'd say our true goodbyes the next morning.

I reached my gate early. I had no idea how early you were supposed to get to the airport before a flight, so I had time to kill. I tried to read one of the books Marcus had given me, but I was too nervous to do much of anything but jiggle my leg anxiously and drum my fingers on the metal armrest beside me. People walked briskly by, trailing suitcases on wheels, bent under the weight of backpacks meant for hiking trips. I wanted to know where each person was going. Were they on their way to someone they loved? Returning to someone they hated? Leaving everything behind? Most people didn't look as if they were leaving everything behind. I slung my bag over my shoulder and walked into the airport bar.

Somehow the place seemed full of regulars, people who'd known and drank around each other for years, though I knew that couldn't be true. The darkness was a welcome change from the glaring fluorescence of the lights in the terminal, though it was still just as loud, and I found an empty stool next to a woman in a suit, drinking a martini. It was pretty early in the morning still. I just ordered a beer. I saw the woman register my presence with a quick, slight look in my direction and I felt embarrassed by my outfit, my choice of drink. Compared to her, I just looked sloppy.

She kept looking over at me until I realized she wasn't judging me, at least not in the way I'd originally thought. Her gaze, made softer and less subtle by the martinis (now I noticed the empty glass beside the other one), lingered on my face, on the skin of my thighs showing through the rips in my jeans. She swiveled toward me, and smiled. She asked where I was headed, and I didn't know quite how to answer that, so instead I just asked her the same question. It was easy not to reveal anything about yourself as long as you asked the right questions of someone else.

Barbara was on her way back to Indianapolis, where she lived—she'd been in Florida for business. "Well, that sounds glamorous," I said, wanting to take it back immediately.

She laughed. "Honey, I'm sitting in an airport sports bar, waiting on a flight that's been delayed... three times now. I barely left the airport hotel the whole time I was here. It's quite far from glamorous."

"But you're doing it," I said. I was jealous. I couldn't imagine having a job that would require me to fly to different cities on a regular basis—that I would ever be considered that important to where my actual presence was needed. "They want you there. In person. It must be a good feeling, to be needed that way."

She smiled, and flagged down the bartender with a gentle wave of her hand. "Another one of these, please? Actually, two." The bartender walked away, and Barbara smacked her forehead playfully. "Here I go again! I just assumed you'd want another drink—and that you'd want what I was drinking. Stupid me." I had an odd desire to comfort her.

"No, no, I like martinis," I said, only half-lying, not even. I wanted to drink this one, at least. If only to please her.

"Thank god," she said, and exhaled with a dramatic whoosh. "Now we know we've got at least one thing in common." She raised her eyebrow at me and smiled. Barbara was flirting with me, I was pretty sure. It was an unsettling feeling. Foreign, but strangely familiar. And even more strange to find myself flirting back. Was I doing it out of habit, on autopilot? Out of a desire to please? Or for my own enjoyment? I was so out of touch that I didn't even know the answer. So I kept talking, just to drown out any doubt that I had.

"Oh, I've been a pharmaceutical rep for years," she said, elbows on the bar, twirling the olive-studded toothpick from her drink between her fingers. "Used to be a man's world, let me tell you. Not so much anymore." I must have looked at her suit, her short hair, for a beat too long, because she added, "I don't need short skirts or long blond hair to make my numbers. I'm that good." *Was* she flirting? I noticed her ring finger was bare.

Barbara was the kind of woman my mom would have made fun of, rolled her eyes after I'd told her about our conversation. "Pathetic," she would have said, an expression of disdain on her face that I'd only recently come to see was strikingly similar to envy. I could hear her as clearly as if she were sitting on my other side, knocking back a beer and whispering sloppily in my ear. "Sure, she gets that paycheck every two weeks, bam. But you really think she's happy, Cal? That kind of job is just going to make you miserable. Stuck at a desk all day; spreadsheets and meetings and phone calls where nobody says what they mean." I wasn't going to listen to her. How would she even know? She'd never worked an office job in her life.

Made bold by the drinks I'd had already, I asked her how her boyfriend felt, if she had one, about her traveling all the time. Barbara laughed loudly. "I don't think I've had a boyfriend since high school," she said. "Not interested."

I pressed further. "Not interested in relationships?" She rotated in her chair, with great effort, it seemed, in order to face me more directly.

"In men," she said, and leaned back defiantly, as if she were waiting for me to act shocked, or disgusted.

"Oh," I said. "Okay." I nodded.

"I'm now sensing. From your reaction." Barbara was punctuating the middle of her sentences now. "That *you*. In fact *are*."

"I am what?"

"Interested in men." She exhaled in a way that made me think of a giant helium balloon losing air. "My fault. I just looked over and saw this beautiful woman, and you were wearing—" she gestured to my baggy jeans, the old t-shirt, the leather jacket hanging over the back of my chair.

I bit my lip. This would be a different kind of rejection, less and more personal at the same time. Yes. I was definitely only interested in men, I reassured myself. "Oh!" I said stupidly, "Yeah, actually. I do like men. I'm sorry, I didn't mean—" Before I could finish, the music changed, and Carly Simon's voice, tinny but loud, began to pump out of the speakers.

Oh, mother, say a prayer for me. I was seized by an anxiety so power-ful that I felt glued to the barstool. I hadn't heard that song in years, not since I'd been in the car with my mom on the way to Eugene for the first time. This was the song we'd been listening to when we hit the rabbit. I felt an irrational fear that something just as sudden was going to happen to me now, on my way to Eugene just like we'd been the first time. Was it a sign? No. I dismissed that immediately. It wasn't a sign. It was just a sudden and unexpected immersion in the past.

"I have to go," I said to Barbara, and threw some money on the bar for my beer. I heard her call after me, in a voice tinted with genuine concern, but I didn't look back. I curled up in a row of empty leather seats by my gate and closed my eyes. I was twelve again, turning up the dial on that car radio, blissfully happy even though I had no idea what we would do next. That had been one of the last moments when my mother would seem like a hero, of any kind, to me.

As a parent, you can try to keep things secret from your chil-dren. You can try to conceal the cracks in your life, the dirty and perpetual work that goes into making life just a little bit better, the cheap and dangerous shortcuts you take to experience some-thing that could almost pass for joy because you're terrified of actually trying to find it, and failing miserably.

But as a child, you see everything. You already have all the pieces, the memories, the fleeting moments you bore witness to but didn't understand. You don't know that you're just waiting for the day when you'll know enough about your own self to assemble them. It won't happen until much later. But when it does, it will feel like finally throwing away a map to a city you've been navigating uncertainly for years.

I willed myself not to cry. This must have been the way she felt. Traveling blindly away from home, putting all her trust in the idea that someone—anyone—would be there. Not even waiting for her, just there. *I could have been a better daughter,* I thought. *I could have been so much better.*

I stayed there long after the song ended, eyes still closed, until it was time to board.

Shoving my bag underneath the seat in front of me, I glanced at my neighbor, a woman already settled in the window seat. She smiled wide, in a friendly way, but also in a way that suggested she was looking for approval, reciprocity, that she'd been smiling like that for so long that it was almost reflexive. I wasn't sure if I was embarrassed for her or jealous of her—I'd been training myself to hide that kind of vulnerability for years.

"Paula," she said, with a heavy Central Florida accent, holding out her hand, impeccably manicured, in a pastel shade of lavender.

"Oh!" I said, and realized she was expecting me to shake her hand, which I did.

"Cal," I said, imitating her. She smiled again and I saw a smudge of lipstick on her front tooth. I didn't say anything. That was the price you paid for vulnerability. She smoothed her denim dress and buckled her seatbelt, taking out a Danielle Steel novel while a flight attendant explained how the oxygen masks worked, how the cushions underneath our seats would double as flotation devices. Upon takeoff, I clutched the armrests so tightly that my fingers took a minute to uncurl. When I took out the safety packet, Paula tapped me lightly on the shoulder, and

I startled, unused to touch. "If it's our time, it's our time," she said. "The Lord does everything for a reason." I wanted to ask her if she really thought that, if she would stay calm if the plane were truly going down, refuse to pull down her oxygen mask, be found amidst the wreckage, dead and bloodied, still buckled in, that serene smile frozen on her face. People were infuriatingly good at knowing what they would do until they actually found themselves in that situation. But I stayed silent. Paula went back to her book.

I'd meant to read on the plane, but after the airport bar and Barbara and my mother's voice in my head, I realized I was flipping pages without absorbing anything, reading the same paragraphs over and over. I wasn't attracted to Barbara. I knew that, probably. But I wondered how many other times my mother's voice had been in my head, quieter, a slight sinister background noise—how many times I'd let her, or my idea of her, make my decisions for me.

I opened my eyes to see the ground slowly approaching through Paula's window. "We'll be landing in about fifteen minutes," the captain announced over the intercom. "Welcome to Eugene." I rubbed my eyes, coming out of the thick fog of a dreamless sleep. I was so close. The wheels slammed down, and we hurtled across the tarmac. I stared past Paula out the window while we waited for the rows in front of us to empty. As we filed off the plane, I had this feeling, like being on the edge of a diving board as a child, with a line forming behind you. You couldn't turn back. You just had to jump, trust that the water would catch you when you dove.

Even though we'd talked on the phone a lot after that first conversation, I was nervous to see Starr. I was supposed to call her from a payphone when my plane landed but before I did that, I found a bathroom by the baggage carousels where I washed my face at the sink, blotting my skin with cheap paper towels that made it rough and reddened. I took out my canister of dry shampoo and sprayed my hairline, flipping my head over and messing up my hair with my hands while I waited for the redness on my cheeks to fade. I still used the same brand of dry shampoo that Starr had handed me in her bathroom years ago. And every time I sprayed it, eyes closed, the scent made me feel like I was back in that bathroom, learning. Happy.

19

I still sleep in the guestroom, except it's not the guestroom any-more, it's my own bedroom, and most nights I'm sleeping in the master bedroom anyway. But it's important to have boundaries, Starr says, and we try not to spend every night together. She's older now, obviously, but she's stopped wearing all that makeup, except for some peachy blush and lipstick on special occasions, and she looks kinder somehow, more relaxed. Her hair is still impeccable.

She lives in the same house, but Russ is gone. "Kicked him to the curb pretty soon after you two went back to Florida," she says with a heavy laugh, one that confirms another thing I didn't want to believe about my mother. Starr's done me the favor of not telling me the exact reason she and Russ broke up, but she didn't have to say anything for me to know it had something to do with that check from Russ that my mom and I drove off with. She's still working out of her house part-time, but now she's doing hair and makeup for the local news station, and every weekday morning for a couple hours she's at the studio, putting bronzer on the female—and male—news anchors, and making sure their hair stays in place the whole time they're on air.

I took the GED in Eugene and got my diploma, and started feeling less like a complete fuck-up. Starr found me a reception-ist job at the news studio where she worked, and we carpooled there in the mornings. "Take your time," she said. "Don't just go out and get another waitress job. Figure out what you want out of life before you go jumping right back in."

On that awful, silent drive back from Eugene years before, my mom had dismissed Starr as a complete idiot. "She's unreal," my mom said. "She has no idea what's going on around her. She lets people walk all over her." I wondered then if my mom was talking about herself, but I didn't ask. I was already in enough trouble. I'd never thought Starr was dumb, but talking to her now, I realized how much good advice she gave, and how much she knew and didn't let on. Just because she'd gone to bed early didn't mean she was oblivious to what had been going on in her living room. "It's easier when you act like you have no clue," she said. "Easier to surprise people. I like that."

She knew I wasn't calling her to escape. I'd already done that. She sent me a plane ticket. "I know you'll pay me back," she said. "Doesn't matter when."

"You'll know where I'm living anyway," I said, and we both laughed. I couldn't remember the last time I'd made a joke about my own life that hadn't made me sad.

I was learning, but Starr was patient and kind and comforting, and being with her felt so much more right than any of the men I'd fucked before. In a way, it was like I'd already had a map of her body for years, just with slightly different proportions, and once I thought about it that way, it felt almost intuitive. "I just love *people*," she said, when I tried to make sense of her romantic past. "It doesn't matter who or what they are." I thought about that for a long time, and the more I thought about it, the more it made sense. You just want someone who makes you feel good.

"You're gonna kick me out of bed when I turn forty," she said once, afterward, as we lay naked and sweaty in her king-sized bed. I laughed, and ran my hand down her stomach, her skin as soft as it had been when I'd zipped up her dress years ago. "Never," I said, and meant it. She traced the constellation on my arm. I leaned over and kissed her, and she pulled me on top of her. Lying on top of Starr, my limbs mirroring hers, I remembered that night on Marcus and Daryl's roof before we'd left Tampa for good, how I'd rolled on top of Marcus in that exact same way. How I'd begged for this exact feeling, too young, from the wrong person. How badly I wanted to be touched. How badly I wanted not to be lonely. Maybe me and Starr weren't the most normal couple on the surface. Maybe it would take me years to figure out what I wanted from life. But I had this.

Starr still does my hair sometimes. She rarely drinks anymore, and never during the day, but sometimes after we've eaten dinner and had a few glasses of wine, we take the rest of the bottle into the living room, leaving all the lights off except for the lamp next to the couch. She sits me down in a chair in front of one of the salon bowl sinks and wraps me in one of those nylon capes, snapping it into place around my neck. And I lean back, eyes closed, and wait for the spray of hot water, for her soft, strong hands to massage that same coconut-smelling shampoo into my scalp, working out the tangles gently, one by one.

Acknowledgments

Many thanks to my friends who read many drafts and iterations of this book, and to those who connected me to their wider community of writer friends, especially Amy Gall and Patty Cottrell. Thank you to Sarah Gerard, for your friendship, your practical advice and assistance, and your quiet confidence in me from the first day we met. I cannot thank you enough for how much you have championed my writing, and especially this book. Thank you to Matt Wise, for your advice early on. A major thank you to Dean Bakopoulos for setting me up with my wonderful agent, Amy Williams. And thank you to Amy, whose enthusiasm was enough for the two of us when it needed to be. It's time for some celebratory coconut cake! Thank you to Eliza Wood-Obenauf and Eric Obenauf for taking a chance on me—in particular, Eric, for your patience and flexibility, and Eliza for the most precise and thoughtful editor I could have asked for.

Thank you to Bryan Thomas, fellow Floridian, for letting me use your beautiful photography on the cover. Thank you to *West 10th*, Bennington's *Plain China*, and *Joyland Magazine* (in particular, Emily Schultz and Brian Joseph Davis) for publishing various bits of this book before it was one, and for making me feel like there might actually be something to it. Thank you to Susan Minot, for your honesty, advice, and book recommendations. Thank you to the entire Greenlight crew, especially Jessica Stockton Bagnulo and Rebecca Fitting, for creating the first space in New York that felt like home to me.

Thank you to Jeff Clanet, for just Getting It. Everything is easier with you, in all the right ways. Thank you to N. Thoma, for knowing what questions to ask. Thank you to Allison, for being my other slice of pizza. Thank you to Lillian Weber and Haley Zoller for your Official Counsel (and for always picking out the jalapeños). Thank you to Camille Drummond and Rumaan Alam, for fielding the bulk of my frantic text messages. Thank you to A, for showing me how it's done.

Thank you to every student and teenager I've worked with over the last few years. You've made me more compassionate and courageous, pressed me to consider my ethical obligations and moral stances outside of the theoretical, and trusted me enough to reveal the most difficult and painful parts of your lives. I couldn't ask for better clients—I only hope that I've done as much good for you as you have for me.

Thank you to my parents, who are—and have always been—incredibly kind, supportive, and generous (and who believe me when I tell them that yes, this is fiction). I don't tell either of you thank you nearly enough. Thank you to my mother in particular, for letting me sit in the back of her bookstore most summers, eating Taco Bell and reading instead of going to camp.

And a final thank you to Florida. I don't know who I'd be if I hadn't had you.

Two Dollar Radio
Books too loud to Ignore

ALSO AVAILABLE Here are some other titles you might want to dig into.

THE UNDERNEATH NOVEL BY **MELANIE FINN**

← *"The Underneath is an excellent thriller."* —*Star Tribune*

THE UNDERNEATH IS AN INTELLIGENT and considerate exploration of violence—both personal and social—and whether violence may ever be justified. With the assurance and grace of her acclaimed novel *The Gloaming*, Melanie Finn returns with a precisely layered and tense new literary thriller.

PALACES NOVEL BY **SIMON JACOBS**

← *"Palaces is robust, both current and clairvoyant… With a pitch-perfect portrayal of the punk scene and idiosyncratic, meaty characters, this is a wonderful novel that takes no prisoners."* —*Foreword Reviews*, starred review

WITH INCISIVE PRECISION and a cool detachment, Simon Jacobs has crafted a surreal and spellbinding first novel of horror and intrigue.

THEY CAN'T KILL US UNTIL THEY KILL US ESSAYS BY **HANIF ABDURRAQIB**

⟶ **Best Books 2017:** NPR, *Buzzfeed*, *Paste Magazine*, *Esquire*, *Chicago Tribune*, *Vol. 1 Brooklyn*, *CBC* (Canada), *Stereogum*, *National Post* (Canada), *Entropy*, *Heavy*, *Book Riot*, *Chicago Review of Books* (November), *The Los Angeles Review*, *Michigan Daily*

← *"Funny, painful, precise, desperate, and loving throughout. Not a day has sounded the same since I read him."*
—Greil Marcus, *Village Voice*

BINARY STAR NOVEL BY **SARAH GERARD**

⟶ *Los Angeles Times* **Book Prize Finalist**

⟶ **Best Books 2015:** *BuzzFeed*, *Vanity Fair*, NPR

← *"Rhythmic, hallucinatory, yet vivid as crystal."* —NPR

AN ELEGIAC, INTENSE PORTRAIT of two young lovers as they battle their personal afflictions while on a road trip across the U.S.

Thank you for supporting independent culture!
Feel good about yourself.

Books to read

Now available at **TWODOLLARRADIO.com** or your favorite bookseller.

Now available at **TWODOLLARRADIO.com** or your favorite bookseller.

THE GLOAMING NOVEL BY **MELANIE FINN**

→ **New York Times Notable Book of 2016**

← "Deeply satisfying." —*New York Times Book Review*

AFTER AN ACCIDENT LEAVES her estranged in a Swiss town, Pilgrim Jones absconds to east Africa, settling in a Tanzanian outpost where she can't shake the unsettling feeling that she's being followed.

THE ONLY ONES NOVEL BY **CAROLA DIBBELL**

→ **Best Books 2015:** *Washington Post*; *O, The Oprah Magazine*; NPR

← "Breathtaking." —NPR

INEZ WANDERS A POST-PANDEMIC world immune to disease. Her life is altered when a grief-stricken mother that hired her to provide genetic material backs out, leaving Inez with the product: a baby girl.

THE INCANTATIONS OF DANIEL JOHNSTON
GRAPHIC NOVEL BY **RICARDO CAVOLO** WRITTEN BY **SCOTT MCCLANAHAN**

← "Wholly unexpected, grotesque, and poignant." —*The FADER*

RENOWNED ARTIST RICARDO CAVOLO and Scott McClanahan combine talents in this dazzling, eye-popping graphic biography of artist and musician Daniel Johnston.

THE REACTIVE NOVEL BY **MASANDE NTSHANGA**

← "Often teems with a beauty that seems to carry on in front of its glue-huffing wasters despite themselves." —*Slate*

A CLEAR-EYED, COMPASSIONATE ACCOUNT of a young HIV+ man grappling with the sudden death of his brother in South Africa.

THE GLACIER NOVEL BY **JEFF WOOD**

← "Gorgeously and urgently written." —*Library Journal*, starred review

FOLLOWING A CATERER AT a convention center, a surveyor residing in a storage unit, and the masses lining up for an Event on the horizon, *The Glacier* is a poetic rendering of the pre-apocalypse.